Running Home

From the Chicken House

It still gives me a shock to read the first few pages – but then Cait and Effie's story is funny too, and so full of love and hope that it made me cry out encouragement to the brilliant sisters and their friends (real *and* imaginary)!
It makes you think about your own family as well – and you might find that you cry a little too. I don't know if there's such a quality as heart-warmingly thrilling, but if there is that's what you have to enjoy here.

Barry Cunningham
Publisher
The Chicken House

Running Home

Teresa Doran

The
Chicken House

2 Palmer Street, Frome, Somerset BA11 1DS

To sisters,
especially mine

Remembering Saturday mornings
at the Irish Writers' Centre

With special thanks to Siobhán,
without whom I might never have started

and to Jonathan
for being there

First published in Great Britain in 2003
The Chicken House
2 Palmer Street
Frome, Somerset BA11 1DF
United Kingdom
www.doublecluck.com

Cover design by Ian Butterworth
Designed and typeset by Dorchester Typesetting Group Ltd
Printed and bound in Great Britain

British Library Cataloguing in Publication data available.

ISBN Hb 1–903434-84-X
ISBN Pb 1–904442-16-1

1 3 5 7 9 10 8 6 4 2

chapter one

She wanted to hug her, but she was afraid. Afraid that if she put her arms around her sister – if she touched her in any way – she would break. She looked so fragile – the veins in her pale cheeks gave her face a porcelain blueness. Above all, Cait was scared that, if she touched Effie, the sudden closeness, that moment of empathy, would cause the two of them to scream, shout, roar crying and behave in such a way she just didn't feel she could cope with. Effie was looking at her, but she wasn't seeing. Her staring eyes were big and round as fat bubbles about to burst. She was clutching the hem of her blue skirt, lifting it up to her face as if to hide. Cait wanted to say something funny: 'I can see your knick-knacks,' but no words would come. Effie's hand was in her mouth, together with a bunch of her skirt. Her fingers glistening wet, the blue material staining dark. Cait had no idea how long they had stood there; it felt like ages and a moment all at once. Silently, Effie pushed her other hand out towards her. Simultaneously Cait's own hand crept down to find that of her sister. Their fingers touched, then palm clutched palm and the screaming started.

The man jerked upright as if he hadn't known they were there. He'd been leaning over their mother like a large black crow. Now he stared at them, wild-eyed, like a total stranger. Fear strangled their crying, and clutching her sister to her, Cait shrank back against the dressing table with Effie's body heaving against hers as she struggled to catch her breath. The feet she could see were her mother's. They stuck out at odd angles off the end of the bed, not moving. But they didn't look like her mother's feet. The bedclothes were all rumpled; she couldn't see her mother's face. Effie was burrowing against her side, one of her shoes had slipped off and she had wet herself. Cait clutched at her tighter as the man approached. The gun was still in his hand, though his arm hung loosely. Cait watched in mesmerised horror as his fingers felt their way around its barrel. He looked at it oddly, as if unsure what it was, what it was for, and what he had just done. He looked down at the two girls trapped like rabbits in the beam of his stare. He raised the gun like a pointing finger. Cait felt her head would explode; the blood pounded in her temples; her mouth was dry. He was looking at them, shaking his head. His lips mouthed a pattern of words: 'I'm sorry. I'm sorry. I'm so sorry.' Suddenly, unpredictably, he turned his hand. The gun cracked and Cait screamed.

'Daaadeeee!'

For a moment there was confusion. The room itself seemed to lurch. The man fell, crashing heavily against an open suitcase that had been pulled out from under the bed. Effie's body jerked, as if she too had been shot and Cait's voice bounced crazily around the ice-green walls, until her scream was swallowed up by the emptiness of silence, until there was no sound louder than the rasp of her breathing. Cait couldn't move. Clutched to her sister, crushed in the corner where the dressing table almost met the wall, she was powerless to even think about what had just happened. Their father had fallen backwards, one arm stretched out towards the wall that was now spattered with his blood. He had shoes on. Their mother's feet were bare. Shoe the little horse. Shoe the little mare. And let the little foal go bare, bare, bare. That was what Mam had said – yesterday.

Yesterday they had gone to the beach. It was a funny sort of beach. Dad had just pulled up at a tiny car park at the side of a road that looked more as if was next to an industrial site than a beach. A battered sign read:

Spit Beach. Take Your Litter Home.
Cornwall County Council.

Mam said it was an odd name for a beach and Effie said there was no beach, she couldn't see the sea. Turned out they had to go down under a railway bridge and along a little path, fenced on both sides. Behind the fence was a factory and all the bushes were dusted white, like they were on the moon or something. Cait asked what it was, and Dad said it was once his bread and butter. Effie made a face and said she wouldn't like to eat it, and Mam laughed and said it was the clayworks. Cait told Effie that Dad used to work for the clayworks. He and his brother, Robert. Long, long ago, before they came to Ireland and he met Mam. She knew Effie probably wouldn't understand. Sometimes Effie thought nothing existed before she was born. It didn't matter anyway. The sun was warm and the trees in their clay dust were kind of Christmassy. Like winter in summer, Cait thought. There was an arrow sign showing where you had to go, and someone had written on it:

Dog Dirt Alley

Mam said that was disgusting, but it was true. Because of the fences people couldn't let their dogs go out under the bushes, so they'd had to do their business there on the path. Cait and Effie counted fourteen dog poos on the way to the beach. Effie said there were fifteen, but Cait said the last one was too small and was probably a seagull dropping, so it didn't really count.

The beach, though, was lovely. The sand was very white and kind of prickly, like granulated sugar, but the tide was out and the browner sand nearer the water was much firmer and cooler to walk on. While Mam spread out their frayed beach mats and set up base, Dad sat on the cool-box, looking out over the sea and the girls put their togs on.

'Will you come swimming?' Cait had asked, but Dad refused.

He looked a bit grumpy as he rolled a cigarette out of his special box, so Cait decided not to ask him again. Mam came down to the water's edge instead. She didn't have her togs, but she took off her sandals and paddled in the water. Satisfied that her daughters were not going to be sucked under by any strong currents and drowned, she went back to Dad. Cait could see she was still watching them, but Dad was looking the other way. They'd swum for a while, until the goose-pimples were standing out on

Cait's arms like the skin of one of Nana's chickens when she plucked it, and Effie's teeth were chattering behind her blue lips, then went back to base for a drink of the lemonade that Mam had brought. Dad didn't speak. He was still sitting, hunched over, drinking from a can of beer and smoking another cigarette. Cait looked the way he was looking and saw two big ships right on the horizon. They looked pretty small to her – she could cover them with one finger – but they were ships, so she knew they must be big.

'They're waiting for the tide so they can come into the port,' Mam said.

'What's the tide?' asked Effie.

'It's when the water comes in and out on the beach.'

'Why?'

'It just does.'

Cait knew Effie didn't understand about tides. Not as much as she did. But then Effie was only six, and she was twice that. Back home in Ireland, there were only lakes near where they lived. When the water was low, it meant it hadn't rained for a while. Usually the water was pretty high. At the beginning of the holiday, when Dad was talking more, he told them to be careful of the tides – that they could cut you off. Effie asked if it would hurt if they cut you, but Dad just laughed and warned them not to go further than he could see.

His laugh had been a nice warm chuckle then. Not like last night, long after she and Effie had gone to bed, when he and Mam had come home and he'd laughed at something Mam had said. It was awful, she could still hear him laughing, but it wasn't an 'oh that's really funny' sort of laugh, it was a horrid sort of bogeyman laugh. Mam had screamed back at him to shut up or he'd wake the children and Cait had put her head under the pillow, waiting for them both to be quiet.

She shut her eyes tight and made herself think again about Spit Beach. She remembered the sunshine and the sand around the neck of the bottle of lemonade they'd drunk from. Then, when they'd quenched their thirst, they'd taken the shrimping nets and a bucket between them and had gone out to explore the rock pools.

'Eeech! Ouch!' they squeaked for every step they took along the barnacle-encrusted rocks.

'Look out for the green seaweed!' Cait had warned. 'It's slippery.' But she was too late, Effie skidded, landing hard on her bottom with a sharp cry that made their mother look over. Cait picked Effie up. She was OK; more shocked than hurt.

At the first pool they filled their bucket with water, and teased their nets along the fringes of weeds at the water's edge. Tiny glass-bright shrimps jerked away from their probing, and when Cait caught one and held up her net to see it, it carried on jumping, and she was amazed that she could see right through it. It was only small, but she put it in the bucket, so that when she caught a bigger one, it wouldn't be lonely. Effie caught a crab next. Only a tiny green one, but they put it in the bucket, too, and straight-away it went scuttling sideways, looking for a corner that wasn't there.

By the time Mam called them back, they had a good few shrimps in their bucket, and when they looked up, the sea had already covered half the rocks and was nearly up to their base.

'That's the tide,' Cait had said knowledgeably to Effie.

They picked their way back over the rocks, carrying their bucket carefully, so they wouldn't spill anything.

'Look, Mam,' Effie said proudly. 'I caught six shrimpies an' a crab.'

Mam peered into the bucket, wrinkling her nose a bit. Cait reckoned she didn't like the seaweed smell up close.

'Bring 'em home,' Dad said. 'Put 'em in boiling water and eat 'em.'

'Daddy!' Effie was horrified.

'Don't be so disgusting,' Mam said.

'''Tisn't disgusting.' Dad drained the dregs from a can of beer. 'If you were hungry, you'd eat them.'

'*You* might,' Mam said, in a way that implied that she wouldn't.

'You'd eat them when you're out. Headless and tailless with a bit of soggy lettuce and pink goo.' Dad put on a silly girly voice that didn't make them laugh, 'Oh please waiter, I'd like a prawn cocktail.'

'That's different.'

'Like hell it is.' Dad threw his empty beer-can over the rock. It rolled with a light clatter and plopped into the sea foam. There were two other empties, half-buried in the sand, their silver metal tops glinting in the late afternoon sun.

Effie stooped to grab. 'Can I throw one?'

'Leave 'em be,' Dad growled. 'Tide'll get 'em.'

He took the bucket then and upended it. With a hiss the water soaked into the white sugar sand and the tiny green crab scuttled into the weed. Translucent bodies flapped helplessly.

'Dad!' Effie cried out. 'They'll be drownded!'

'They'd be dead anyway.' Flicking his jacket over his shoulder and side-spitting the cigarette butt from his mouth, Dad turned and crunched his way up the beach. Shouldering the bags, Mam followed him, and since she had all the stuff put away, Cait and Effie kept their togs on.

Nobody said anything to anybody all the way back to the car park, along the narrow path between the high fences. Cait silently counted the fourteen dog poos and the small one that might have been a seagull dropping. Dad opened the boot and slammed it shut, so quick after Mam put the stuff in she had to jump back. Cait sat down to put on her sandals, while Mam took Effie on to her lap to put on hers. She rubbed the sand off Effie's feet so she wouldn't be sore.

Effie laughed because it tickled and Mam sang: 'Shoe the little horse. Shoe the little mare. And let the little foal go ...'

'Bare, bare, bare,' sang Effie.

Cait opened her eyes a fraction. She couldn't hold on to yesterday any more. Her Mam's feet were still bare. Dad's feet had their shoes on. Why? Why? Why? She had started to shake, like she was freezing, yet she was nearly stuck to her sister's side with the sweat of the two of them. Effie wasn't moving. Cait gently peeled her away. Effie looked up at her sister, her blonde fringe dark and plastered to her forehead. Her cheek was creased and patterned where it had pressed against Cait's shirt.

'Cait,' she whispered. 'I want to go home.'

chapter two

'OK,' said Cait, reassuringly stroking her sister's head. 'We'll go home.'

Carefully she unfolded her legs. The pins and needles had made them feel all wobbly. Standing, trying not to shake, she pulled her sister up to her and together they tiptoed from the room as if afraid to disturb the motionless, sprawled bodies of their parents. Cait closed the door quietly. It mightn't be so bad if they couldn't see. Now they were in the kitchen of their holiday bungalow. It looked normal. The paper was still open on the table at the sports page. Plates and crumbs and knives with eggy blades were scattered around as if the reader of the paper had simply pushed them aside.

'You thirsty?' Cait asked.

Effie nodded.

Cait went to the fridge. There was not much except two cans of beer and the plastic remains that all the others had been pulled from. There was a half-carton of milk, though, and Cait filled a small glass and gave it to her sister.

'Drink up. It's good for you,' she said automatically.

She began to clear the table. They couldn't sit at a table that was covered in dirty crockery. She folded the paper, piled up the dishes and placed them in a heap in the sink. Maybe she would wash them later. She poured herself some milk and sat down opposite her sister.

'We should call the guards.'

Effie looked up questioningly. A moustache of milk framed her mouth. She said nothing.

'Guards. Police. Or whatever they call themselves over here.'

Effie was suddenly alarmed. 'No guards.' She stared hard into her half-empty glass, biting her lip. 'No police. Dad said.'

Cait understood. The police were pigs, Dad said. Mean-minded and always out to get you. They were out to get him, Dad said. All the time. They had a way, Dad said, of asking you questions like they wanted to be your friend, but all the time they were trying to catch you out. Tell 'em nothing, Dad said. Don't even look in their direction. Mam called the police once. She'd locked Dad out of the house and he was roaring and kicking, trying to get back in. She and Effie had hidden under the bed in their room. When the police came, they wouldn't come out, but Mam said they had to, that Dad was quiet now, and the police only wanted to talk to them. But Mam lied, or the police lied. They didn't just want to talk to them; they wanted to bring them away. Dad said he wouldn't let them go. He'd kill them before he'd let the police take them; before he'd let *anyone* take them. He stabbed the air with a knife to show he meant business, and Cait screamed, even though she knew the knife was the one from the kitchen and blunt because Mam used it to clean out the plughole.

It was useless as a knife, but the police didn't know that. They took hold of Dad, while a policewoman led her and Effie outside with blankets wrapped round them because it was cold and night-time. Cait remembered how Mam had cried – a cry that was more like the roar of a weanling cow they'd hear from the fields next to Nana's – as she and Effie were put into a car. Not one with a flashing-light, just an ordinary car, that brought them to another family that wasn't their family. They could have taken them to Nana's, or even found Uncle Robert, Dad's brother. For even though she had seen him only now and again, Cait remembered he was always there for them, nice – and funny. She was sure he'd have looked after them. But the police knew best – they said – and took them to a family of strangers. She was nice enough, the mother, but she wasn't their mother. Effie hardly spoke the whole time they were with this other family. Cait knew they thought she was stupid – she overheard the mother and father talking one evening. But Effie wasn't stupid. She might have only been four, but she could talk quite well, when she wanted to. She just didn't want to. That was all.

But now she should tell *someone*, all the same, Cait reasoned. Whatever Dad might have said. That was what you were supposed to do when something really bad happened.

'Maybe someone will come.' Cait was thinking aloud. 'Maybe someone heard.' She looked anxiously out the window. The cattle were making their way down the field to the water-trough, just as they had done every evening since the family had been there. The sky was still a scalding blue. It was as hot today as it had been yesterday when they went to the beach. Probably everyone else had gone to the beach again. They hadn't gone today, because Dad wanted to watch football on the TV. It was very quiet. Maybe there was no one else around.

'I wish we never came to Cornwall,' Effie suddenly spoke. 'I wish we went to Nana's.'

Cait nodded. 'Me too.'

Every summer they went to Nana and Granda. Except *this* summer they took the car, crossed on the ferry and drove all the way to Cornwall. It had been such an adventure. Neither of them had ever been on a boat bigger than Granda's currach, and it had been great fun going up and down the stairs and trying to stand up without wobbling. Effie had found a pound, left behind in one of the fruit machines. She was so small that it was easy for her to look in the shelf that gives out the money. They'd used it to have a go at a racing-car game together, but the money ran out before they'd even got the hang of driving the cars well enough to make a second turn. They didn't even mind the long drive down to Cornwall, and when they weren't asleep they passed the time by counting motorway bridges. Cait counted the curved ones and Effie the straight. She couldn't remember how many they'd counted, but there had been an awful lot. It was evening time when they finally arrived at 'Happy Meadows', but being summer, there was still plenty of time to go and explore. They found the swimming pool, the games room and the little library where you could borrow jigsaw puzzles as well as books. Effie had picked a bunch of daisies to brighten up their holiday bungalow, but as soon as she put them in a little vase – an egg-cup – their stems flopped until their sunny bright faces touched the formica table-top. She had grabbed the bunch in disgust and fed it to the cattle in the field beside them. Oh yes. It had been such an adventure coming to Cornwall, but now she wished they had gone to

Nana's instead. Effie had dripped a bit of milk on the table and was making swirly patterns in it with her finger.

'We could ring Granda and he'd come and fetch us.'

'Don't be silly,' Cait dismissed the idea. 'Granda can't drive.'

Granda didn't even own a car. Cait doubted if he or Nana had ever driven a car in their lives. Granda had a big black bike with high handlebars that took him wherever he wanted to go. Nana's bike was the same, but with a basket in front. When Effie was very small she fitted right into the basket and with Cait on the crossbar of Granda's the four of them could go for a ride together. Nana and Granda lived in New Quay, County Clare. It was a tiny place, yet they said they would rather live there than anywhere else. Mam once asked them to come and stay, but they said, 'No, thank you. What would we do in a great big town with no grass and too much noise? We're managing fine where we are.' Dad said, 'Let 'em stew,' which Cait had thought funny, particularly as Nana's stew was her absolute favourite thing to eat. Her stomach was rumbling. She felt hungry. Either hungry or sick, she wasn't sure yet.

Last week Dad brought them to Newquay in Cornwall. He said to Mam, 'What would they think to *this* Newquay?' He thought it terribly funny and laughed so much he got into a fit of coughing and had to go into a pub to buy a can of beer to soothe his throat, and another for the bird, he said, that never flew on one wing. Cait had agreed with Mam. She thought Nana's New Quay was much nicer. This place was full of people, roaring and shouting. The beach was nice, though, with sand as soft as cement powder and flat all the way to the waves. As a treat, Mam had let them go round the Sea-Life Centre. They went on their own because Dad said the adult tickets were a rip-off price and that he and Mam would wait outside. Cait took Effie by the hand the whole way around, in case she got scared, but she wasn't one bit frightened, even when they walked through the glass tunnel with the sharks swimming over their heads.

Cait came to her senses with a start, her skin prickling. She had the distinct feeling that something – or someone – had brushed past her. A shudder wracked her body, as through a veil of sweat and unfallen tears, she saw the door was open. Not the bedroom door – she'd shut it earlier – but the one to the outside. Cait stood up, crossed the room painfully – pins and needles again had turned her legs to wood – and nervously looked outside. There was no one. Perhaps it was the wind. Perhaps she'd never shut it. The evening was growing cooler, so she closed it now, looking over at her sister. Effie was asleep. Her head had fallen forward on to the table, her cheek resting in the spilt milk, her mouth a fraction open, blowing tiny bubbles. At least, Cait thought, she is alive. She wondered how she hadn't noticed the sun going down, and now barely remembered what she'd been thinking about. She could hear faint sounds: voices; a ball bouncing. Other people must have come back from wherever they'd been today. Funny, she thought, she didn't remember hearing any cars. Nobody had come. She was sure of that. Nobody had found them; though she half-wished they had. But it was late now, already getting dark.

'Effie,' she whispered, 'it's bed-time.' She said it again, louder, startling herself with the sound of her voice in this room that was more silent than a grave. Effie twitched, made little grunting sounds, and slowly her eyes unglued themselves.

'Bed-time, Effie.' Cait tried to sound normal. Say it the

same way as last night. The way she always said it when Mam and Dad would go out and she'd mind her sister and put her to bed. Like a robot, Effie climbed down from the chair and let Cait guide her to the bedroom they shared. Sticking out her arms and legs when asked, she let Cait undress her, only flinching when Cait accidentally touched the still-livid bruises from when she'd fallen on the rocks. The clothes were wet and smelly and Cait took them to the dirty-clothes pile in the bathroom when she went to fetch a flannel to clean her sister's face. Dressed in a night-gown with three rabbits on the front that used to be Cait's, Effie climbed sleepily into bed. Her hand flapped around on the pillow, sightlessly searching.

'Mi Mi.'

Cait froze. Mi Mi was a floppy pink bunny. Dad had won it at a fair when Effie was about two, and she had got so excited she'd held out her arms calling 'Me, me, me, me,' over and over. The name had stuck and since then Effie had taken it with her almost everywhere. She had it, Cait remembered, when they were playing on the steps outside and went to investigate the noises coming from their parents' bedroom, and now, like the image that was burnt into the back of her eyes, she saw it fallen, face-down, just by the leg of the dressing table.

'Mi Mi's not here just now.' She steadied her voice. 'Can you sleep without him?'

'Want Mi Mi.' Effie began to pull herself into a sitting position. Cait calmed her.

'OK. I'll get Mi Mi. I know where he is. You just wait there.'

Effie nodded. She was waiting.

'I'll just go and get him.' Cait backed out of the door, leaving it just a little ajar. The other bedroom door was

still closed and she stood outside, her hand on the knob, gathering her thoughts and steadying her breath.

'There's no one in there. There is no one in there,' she told herself over and over again, running through in her mind the exact position of the bed, the window and the dressing table. 'There is no one.' She opened the door a crack. Nothing happened. A little further. Still nothing. She kept her eyes fixed to the floor. The triangular shaft of light from the kitchen jumped in size as she opened the door a little wider. In the point of the light lay Mi Mi, just at the foot of the dressing table. Holding her breath she tiptoed in, never letting her gaze leave the fluffy pink rabbit. She grabbed it and ran, shutting the door swiftly and silently behind her as she breathed again.

Effie was asleep. Cait tucked the rabbit in beside her and sat on the side of the bed. What would she do now? Nothing had changed. Mam and Dad were still in their room. She and Effie were still on their own. She hadn't told anyone. But how could she? No one had come, and the telephone she might have used was up in that library place. She couldn't have gone there. She couldn't have gone and left Effie here on her own; and it was too late now. She closed the curtains, shutting out the night. Maybe in the morning.

She envied her sister's peaceful sleep as she took her night-dress out from under the pillow of her own bed. She changed quickly, her teeth chattering even though it wasn't particularly cold. She turned back her sheet, but hesitated. Tonight was not the night to be alone. Carefully, so as not to awaken her sister, she slipped in behind Effie and hugged her.

Morning brought another blue-skied day. The warmth of

the sun was already penetrating the flimsy curtains when Cait sleepily opened her eyes. She shivered, as if waking after a bad dream, and wondered why she was lying tight up against her still-sleeping sister. But it was the lack of noise elsewhere that disturbed her. Usually Mam would be up by now. There should be a smell of tea and toast. She crept out of bed and gingerly entered the kitchen. It was just as it had been yesterday afternoon. It was as if time had not moved on.

'Mam,' she called softly – hopefully.

There was nothing. Outside seemed to stretch with a morning laziness, but inside there was nothing. Except for the muffled buzzing of a fat bumblebee as it smashed repeatedly into the window above the sink, there was silence. The door to her parents' room was still closed, and with one awful, stomach-churning lurch, Cait knew she had not been dreaming. Suddenly weak, she staggered to the outside door and flung it open. A burst of sun and the loud hum of grasshoppers flooded in to attack the stagnant air inside. Cait leaned over the rail of the wooden patio and tried to force herself to vomit.

'It'll be better, once it's out,' she heard the voice of her mother say.

But it wouldn't come. The sickness she felt was deeper than the pit of her stomach. Rising like a stinking cloud it enveloped her, overwhelmed her. She felt dizzy. Clutching one of the upright poles, she slid to the ground, sitting with her legs dangling over the edge.

'Mornin'!'

A cheery holiday-maker, gaily dressed in bright shorts and with a vivid red towel slung over his shoulder waved up at her as he passed their bungalow. Cait struggled to regain enough of her startled composure to wave feebly back.

'Nice day, innit?' he called back over his shoulder.

'Yeah,' said Cait. 'Nice.'

She could have told him, she thought. Then the tiniest of sounds from within the bungalow startled her, and in an instant she was on her feet. Effie! She always went into their room for a snuggle in the mornings. Cait sprang back into the kitchen. Effie stopped, one hand on the door knob, the other trailing Mi Mi.

'Effie, come here a minute,' Cait tried not to let panic raise her voice.

Obediently, Effie came and Cait led her outside. Side by side, the two sisters dangled their legs over the edge of the patio. Effie said nothing, but kind of sighed, as if she expected her sister to say something. Cait knew what she had to say. She was going to tell Effie to come to the phone with her, so she could call the police. But what then? Suppose they were taken away like the last time? They'd be put into care. Effie would *hate* that. Right now her sister was looking up at her, still waiting. She *couldn't* do that to Effie, who only wanted *her*, Cait, to mind her, not some make-believe mother like you'd get in a Home.

'Do you remember yesterday?' she said instead, quietly.

Effie nodded. She kept her gaze straight ahead. Cait watched her profile from the corner of her eye, trying to gauge her reaction.

'About Mam and Dad?'

Effie nodded again. More slowly this time. Two slow nods, nothing more. Cait knew. Effie wouldn't speak until she felt like talking, but Cait knew.

'We'd better get dressed.' It was just her and Effie now, Cait resolved. And that was how it would stay.

Effie turned her face to Cait's, one eye squinting in the sun.

'We can't stay all day in our 'jammies. Besides ...' Cait drew a deep breath, 'you said yesterday, you wanted to go home.'

Effie nodded. Just once. Very, very slowly. With the hem of her night-dress, Cait wiped her sister's face, drying the swelling tear, just before it fell.

After dressing, Cait suggested they had breakfast, as they had a long journey ahead of them.

'Krispies or toast?'

'Krispies.'

This was a fortunate choice, for when Cait opened the bread-bin there was nothing, except half a packet of stale cream-crackers. She poured Krispies into two bowls and carefully divided the little bit of milk that was left. After they had finished, she cleared the table and put their dirty bowls on top of the other dishes in the sink.

'We'll need some clothes.' Cait was thinking aloud. Together the two girls pulled stuff out of the drawers in their room. Cait decided she would bring her swimming bag and her bum-bag and that Effie could wear her 'My Little Pony' rucksack.

'We won't be able to carry much,' Cait said as she noticed Effie's pile growing bigger and bigger. 'We should bring lots of knickers though. We have to have clean knickers. A spare pair of shorts perhaps. A couple of T-shirts and our toothbrushes. And a jacket, in case it gets cold.'

Effie nodded in silent agreement.

'But no books,' Cait said, noticing Effie about to secrete a couple in her bag. 'Books will be too heavy.'

Reluctantly Effie put the books to one side.

'Oh Effie,' Cait said. 'They weren't even your books

anyway. That's stealing.' Effie looked suitably hangdog and Cait suddenly had an idea. 'Tell you what. Since we won't be needing them, maybe you could take them back to the little library place.'

Effie nodded enthusiastically. Cait sensed it would do her good to get out for a while.

'OK then. But mind you come straight back, and don't talk to anyone. Understand?'

'Yes,' Effie said in a very small voice.

'No talking.'

'No.'

'Here you go then.'

Cait watched Effie make her careful way down the wooden steps, the books held out before her. She didn't really want to be alone, but she had things to do and it would be better if Effie wasn't there. Effie waved from the bottom of the steps and Cait waved back. She didn't have much time. Effie would only be gone a few minutes. Gingerly, she opened the door of her parents' bedroom, taking a couple of deep breaths to steady herself. She would have to imagine they weren't there, just like last night. She thought that if she imagined they were outside in the sun, she could pretend that it was only their clothes left behind on the floor and on the bed. She closed her eyes – made herself believe – then opened them and stepped into the room. She knew what she was looking for and went straight to the dressing table. For a moment she hesitated. Her mother's handbag was out of bounds.

'If you go near your mother's bag,' she could hear her father's voice ringing in her ears, 'I'll clout you so hard, you'll never forget.'

'Dad's not here,' she told herself. 'He can't see me.'

Opening the bag she took out the purse, flicked it open

and tipped the contents on to the table. An English £5 note and a handful of coins, some of them Irish. That wouldn't get them very far. She rooted deeper into the bag. There was a notebook, a small address book, a few tissues (some used), a biro, a packet of tampons, half a packet of Polos, a few bits of make-up, a pair of sunglasses and an old photograph of the four of them. Cait was wearing the white dress she'd worn for her First Communion. Effie was only a baby, and Dad was smiling, holding her. He must have been tickling her, because Effie's body was stiff, leaned back against his shoulder, her mouth open with laughing. Cait smiled to herself. Dad had a way of tickling, just in the soft bit behind the knee that made you go crazy. You couldn't help yourself. You'd be sitting on his lap, or up in his arms and he'd start. He'd be ever so gentle, yet you'd feel like your legs were on fire. He'd do it to her sometimes; even to Mam, when she'd be sitting on his knee, watching telly. She'd laugh so much, she'd go tomato red. But that was then. Years ago. When things were good. If only they could have stayed like that for ever. Sighing, Cait quickly slipped it into her bum-bag, along with the money, the tissues and biro, the make-up and the sweets.

Dad's jacket hung over the back of the chair. Cait took it by the collar and shook it gently. The pockets rattled and felt satisfyingly heavy. She dipped her hand into one and drew out his wallet. It was fatter than Mam's purse at least, and when she opened it, her eyes nearly popped at the number of notes stuffed inside. There were tens, twenties and even two or three fifties.

'Wow,' she breathed, as she kissed the wallet lightly and put it in her bum-bag. In his other pocket she found his special tobacco tin, lighter and the car keys. She opened the tin and took a quick sniff. She wanted to remember Dad's smell. However, the tin was almost empty and the tobacco didn't smell a bit like it did when it was burning. She put it back, but took the lighter – it might be useful – and the car keys just gave her an idea.

Having taken what she needed, she closed the door again. Leaving her bum-bag on the table, she went outside, down the wooden steps, to where the car was parked. She looked briefly around, but told herself not to be silly, no one would take any notice of her, it was *their* car. It wasn't as if she was thinking of stealing it or anything. Sitting in the driver's seat, with the keys in the ignition, she twisted the steering wheel and felt for the pedals. They were miles away! She was small for her age and when she finally stretched out her foot sufficiently, she found she could barely look over the dashboard. That idea wouldn't work after all and anyway, she told herself firmly, they could be easily followed in a car. They'd know the numberplate. She'd seen how they did it on the police crime programmes. Then, of course, there was the small problem of not having a clue how to drive. Dad made it look so easy, but she bet it wasn't. Besides, she had Effie to look after now, so she'd better not do anything dangerous.

A knock on the window startled her. Effie was back. She opened the passenger door and let her sister in.

'Are you going to drive us home?'

'I don't think so.'

'Good.'

'Why?' Cait was perplexed.

''Cause you can't drive, anyways.'

Effie was rooting in the glove compartment. Like a squirrel looking for nuts, she was always rooting for something. She found a tin of travel sweets with three left. They took one each and Cait let Effie have the last one because she had found them.

'What else is in there?' Cait peered into the darkness of the glove compartment – the little light had never worked. She found a map and, opening it, spread it over the steering wheel. 'Look where we are.'

Effie, who had been licking the last of the icing sugar from the bottom of the tin, looked over. Cait pointed to a spot halfway down into Cornwall. 'We're here. And ...' She let her finger trail up through England and Wales, over the sea, across Ireland, landing at a point on the west coast, 'Nana's house is here.'

Effie looked interested, peering over as if she expected to see the house, chimney pots and all, right there on the map.

'Lick your fingers,' said Cait. 'And you've got icing sugar on your nose.'

Cait retraced with her finger the way they had come: Dublin, Holyhead and then down through England. She remembered some of the names from the signs as they passed them by: Birmingham, Bristol, Taunton, Exeter and Plymouth. It really wasn't that far. Two hand-spans from Cornwall to Clare. Dad had managed to find the way here, only getting lost once. Surely she and Effie could find their way back again?

'Come on, Effie,' Cait folded up the map. 'It's time to go.'

'You can't drive.'

'No, I'm not driving. We'll find another way.'

'OK.'

Cait took the map and locked the car. Back in the bungalow they arranged their bags and belongings on the table. Cait tucked Mi Mi into Effie's bag and zipped it.

'We don't want to lose him, do we?'

Putting the bag on her sister's back, she adjusted the shoulder-straps. 'Is that all right?' Effie nodded. 'Not too heavy?' Effie shook her head and, satisfied, Cait shouldered her own bag, fastened the bum-bag around her waist and pulled her shirt down to hide it. Only the car keys were left on the table, and they wouldn't be needing them. Cait looked around briefly. So this was it, she thought.

'Right,' she said, as matter-of-factly as she could. 'Are we ready? Have we got everything?'

'What about Mam and Dad?'

Cait looked towards the closed bedroom door. 'Well, we can't exactly bring them.'

Effie's eyes began to fill with tears. 'But we can't leave them like that.'

Cait had to agree. It didn't seem right. Up till now, she had managed to keep up the pretence that they were not really there, but now Effie had just pricked that bubble of illusion. They really *were* in there, and she and Effie were just going to walk out and leave them.

'But what are we going to do?'

'When Blackie died we buried her,' Effie suggested.

Under the circumstances, Cait thought, burial was out of the question. 'You remember how you cried when Blackie died?'

Effie said she did.

'And you remember how Mam told you not to be sad; that Blackie was already in pussycat heaven, that she was as beautiful and as bouncy as she always was, and that we were to remember her that way and not dead, and we were only burying her mortal body she didn't need any more?'

30

'But we did bury her mortal body,' Effie insisted. 'And we said prayers.'

'We did,' Cait agreed. 'In a hole. Under the apple tree. But we've no hole here, and no apple tree, so we'll just have to pretend.'

Effie was not convinced.

'Listen,' Cait crouched down, taking her sister's hands in hers. 'We'll say that the room in there is the hole, that this place here is the apple tree. And look ...' Cait had spotted a black marker on the floor by their bedroom door, 'We'll put up a cross.' She jumped up and drew a black cross as high as she could reach on the door to their parents' room. Beneath it she wrote R.I.P. 'Is that OK?'

'We have to say prayers now.'

'All right. Who shall we pray to? Holy God or Holy Jesus? You say.'

'Holy Mary,' Effie said with some resolution, placing her palms together and adopting a beatific expression Cait suddenly thought suited her.

'Holy Mary it is, then.' Cait put her hands together. 'Let us pray. Holy Mary, full of grace. Pray for us and our mam and our dad at this hour and for the hour that we shall meet again. Holy Mary look after Mam and Dad and don't let God be too hard on them when he does the judging. Look after me and Effie too and thanks for everything.' Cait hoped that would be enough and that the one prayer would do for the two of them. Even though Dad's God wasn't Catholic, she was sure he wouldn't mind, under the circumstances. Cait looked at Effie, her expression inviting her to say her own piece.

'Amen,' Effie said simply.

chapter three

Nobody saw them leave 'Happy Meadows', or if they did, they took no notice of two girls with small bags and their jackets tied to the straps, apparently out for a stroll between the ornamental hedges of the driveway. In only a few minutes after leaving the bungalow, Cait and Effie were walking along the verge of the main road, the sun on their backs and their bare legs brushed by the wiry stems of rye grass and timothy.

'Where are we going?' Effie skip-jumped to keep up with her sister.

'We'll go to town. There's bound to be a bus stop in town.'

To Cait, the town seemed a sensible place to start their journey. They had been there a couple of times and soon they arrived at the fancy gate that marked the pedestrianised area. Beyond it, the narrow street thronged with people: fat people, thin people, family groups and couples; some with babies carried high on shoulders. It seemed to Cait as if half of Cornwall had gathered here in the town.

'Stick by me,' she commanded. 'Don't get lost.'

Effie clutched at her sister's hand. She would obey.

'Don't talk to anyone neither,' Cait said. 'Don't even look at anyone.'

Hand in hand they made their way up the main street, past Woolworths, Boots and Stead and Simpson, weaving their way through the crowd that took no notice of them other than to make complaint if their paths collided: 'Bloody kids,' 'Watch where you're going!' 'Tchh! Really!' Feeling more buffeted than Granda's currach in a head-wind, Cait steered them towards one of the ornamental flower beds in the centre of the street.

'My legs are tired.' Effie flopped down onto an iron bench. 'What's for lunch?'

Cait didn't have a clue, but a Burger King over the road gave her an idea. 'Chips and burgers?'

Effie licked her lips, 'And a coke.'

Cait fiddled under her shirt for a note out of the bum-bag, and instructing her sister to wait, bought burgers for them both. Oblivious to the crowd milling around them, the girls sated their hunger, reducing the food to crumbs and greasy tissue in a matter of minutes. Effie licked her fingers with relish and belched loudly. Cait let out a gig-gling squeak as an elderly woman, dragging a shopping basket on wheels, looked hard at the two of them. It wasn't funny, she thought. She shouldn't be laughing. It didn't even feel like it was her that was laughing. She was losing control.

'Come on,' she said to her sister. 'We'd better go.'

At the other end of the pedestrian area, a Hopper bus was disgorging its passengers. Cait knew this local shuttle service between the town, beaches and outlying villages was no good to those who wanted to go far away, but she hadn't seen any other bus yet. She approached the driver.

'Excuse me. Are there any other buses, besides these Hoppers?'

'There's the regular service.'

'And where would I find that?'

The man was bored and hot. He barely even looked at Cait. 'Depot's at the top of that hill. By the train station. Can't miss it.'

'Thank you.'

The man swatted a fly off his bald head as he pressed the button that closed the door. Cait stepped back as the Hopper bus pulled away. Train station, she thought. As far as she could remember, they had passed a railway terminus in Holyhead. She patted at the bulge under her shirt. This was going to be easier than she'd thought. 'Come on,' she said to Effie. 'We'll go home by train.'

The road to the station was steep and pulled at the backs of their legs, but the thought of being able to sit down on a seat in a train made them persevere. Sure enough, at the top of the hill, behind the iron railings, a train sat, wheezing like a tamed dragon. As if running to queue for a fairground ride, the girls rushed into the dank coolness of the station building and took their place in a line, behind a wide woman in a green skirt, squeezing each other's hands and grinning inanely.

'Won't Nana be surprised to see us,' Cait whispered.

Then it was their turn. The ticket man peered down through the wire mesh of his booth.

'Yes?'

'Two tickets to Holyhead,' Cait could barely contain her excitement. 'One way.'

'No through trains to Holyhead, my love. You could take one and change at Bristol, Birmingham and Crewe.

Or wait for the Birmingham one and change there and at Crewe.'

'What's that train there?' Cait indicated the one she could still see standing at the station.

'That's the Plymouth train, my love.'

'Could we take that?'

'You'd have to change at Plymouth, Exeter, Bristol, Birmingham and Crewe.'

Cait rummaged in her bum-bag. 'How much?'

The man peered closer at the two of them. 'It's for yourselves, is it?'

Cait nodded.

'How old's your sister?'

'She's six.'

'Well, let me see. She'd be half-price then. If she was five she'd be free, but she's not, so she's half-price. And yourself?'

'Half-price too.'

'But what age are you?'

'Thirteen. Almost.'

The man smiled and shook his head. 'Where's your mother, my love?'

'She's …' Effie was about to say something, but Cait stood on her toe and crossed her fingers under the counter. 'She's in the bathroom.'

'So you'll be needing a ticket for her as well?'

'Yes. Yes, I suppose we would.'

The man smiled. Not a sneery smile, but a nice smile. He folded his hands over his ticket counter. 'Now, suppose we wait and let your mother buy the tickets herself.' Cait felt her heart flop to the level of her shoes. 'See, I can't rightly sell you two tickets, when neither of you is over sixteen, see. Your mother would have to be here … or your father.'

'OK.' Cait tried not to appear crestfallen. 'I'll tell her to come herself, so.'

'How are you going to get her?' Effie hissed as Cait led her smartly away.

'From the bathroom.' Cait smiled sweetly at the ticket man. 'Which way to the Ladies'?'

'Out on the platform. Round to your right. Next please.'

Cait and Effie marched out on to the platform, wheeled right and pushed open the heavy door of the 'Ladies' Rest Room'.

'What now?'

'I don't know yet. Let me think.'

Effie was looking out through the dust-streaked window. 'I think that train is going soon. I think I saw it move.'

Cait pressed her face to the window. The train was at the other platform. They would have to cross the little wooden bridge. There didn't appear to be anyone on this side. 'Let's run for it!'

They sneaked out of the door. A couple of men in suits were just running up the steps to the bridge. 'Come on,' Cait encouraged Effie, and taking her hand they sprinted under the wooden awning and up the steps, their feet pounding on the worn boards.

'Wait!' A man, standing in the centre of the bridge stopped them. He was wearing a uniform. 'Can I see your tickets?'

The girls came to a sliding halt. 'Mam has them,' Cait puffed. 'She's just gone over ahead of us.'

The man was shaking his head. 'You kids must think I was born yesterday.'

Cait grinned. 'Only messing.' Grabbing Effie's hand

again, she spun her round and together the girls pounded back they way had come.

Outside in the sunshine they came to a panting halt near an overgrown footpath at the back of the station.

'Did he come after us?' Cait was bent forward, her knees wrinkled where her hands pressed down on them.

Effie looked back. 'Don't see him.'

Cait straightened up, leaned for a moment against the high wire netting that separated the footpath from the railway track and slumped to the ground. Dejected, her fingers absently plucked at the tufts of scrubby grass.

'You'll get ants in your pants,' Effie said.

'Don't care.' Cait tossed a scraw of grass at the corrugated wall that bordered the other side of the path. It smashed in a satisfying burst of dry pebbles and dust.

'Mam says you will.'

Cait looked up at Effie with one of her old 'she'll have to catch me first' expressions, and Effie sat down promptly beside her sister. They both heard the wheezing creak as the Plymouth train clunked forward and left the station, gathering speed until its rattley-clack was swallowed up by high banks and distance.

'What are we going to do now?'

'Don't know. That man in the station will be looking out for us now. We can't buy tickets because he knows my age. And I lied to him.'

Effie pointed to the white National Express buses lined up beside the double-deckers on the far side of the car park. 'Couldn't we still get a bus?'

'They'd probably say the same thing.' In spite of the burger, Cait felt empty inside, but she tried to smile when Effie handed her a dandelion she'd just picked. 'Thanks,' she said.

'Old pissybed,' Effie said.

'Yeah,' agreed Cait, tearing the yellow petals to shreds.

Effie stood up. 'Get up, lazybones.' Then, adopting a stance with her legs slightly apart and her hands on her hips, just the way Mam would. 'I haven't got all day.'

'Yeah,' Cait wiped her hands on her shorts. 'You're right. Maybe we will try the buses.'

Shouldering their bags, they made their way back along by the chain-link fence in the shadow of the station building. They had now only to cross the car park between the station and the bus depot. Passing by a white van, Cait stopped and hissed.

'It's him!'

Effie stopped, then peered around the back of the van. The station guard was standing in the sun just at the station entrance. He was talking to another man, but both stood looking out over the car park.

'He'll see us for sure,' Cait whispered.

'Then he'll tell the bus driver.'

'He'll tell the police.'

'We'll be put into care!'

'Let's wait.'

Crouched down at the rear of the van they could just see the top of the guard's head. He was still talking – still looking out. He didn't show any sign of leaving. Effie was tracing her initials in the dust of the van.

'Don't,' Cait flicked her sister's hand away.

'It needs a wash, anyways.'

Cait agreed. The van was pretty mucky. Beneath the film of caked dirt, she could just make out the green lettering. 'Evans and Son. Bristol'. The name was suddenly familiar. All the trains to Holyhead seemed to change at Bristol. If they took a ride in this van they could get out at

Bristol and somehow catch a train from there. At least the station guards wouldn't know them in Bristol. The two men were still talking, but they were looking the other way now. She stood up carefully to inspect the van. At the back, it was a sort of truck. It didn't have doors that locked, but it didn't have a roof either. All it had was a kind of tarpaulin cover that was tied down around the edges. There was a rope that went around through eyelet holes at the bottom of the cover and was looped over anchorage pins on the van body. Cait managed to prise one of the loops off and, on tip-toe, she peered inside. She hoped there wouldn't be anything nasty or smelly. Much as she wanted to get home, she didn't feel desperate enough yet to want to ride in anything too horrid.

Effie was pulling at her leg. 'What are you doing?'

'Just looking.'

'Let me see.'

'Wait.'

'What's in there?'

It took Cait a moment to work out the shapes in the darkness. The tarpaulin was a very dark blue and with the sun trying to shine through it, everything inside was sort of dark and purplish. At least it wasn't smelly. As far as she could tell there were rolls of something lined up lengthways along the body of the truck. They looked like some sort of material. She wasn't sure. Leastwise, they weren't metal. Metal would have been cold for two girls to lie on. It was warm inside. The sun saw to that. Pulling her head out from under the cover, Cait crouched down beside her sister.

'Effie, let's play a game.'

'I want to see inside.'

'You will. But first let's pretend we're bank robbers on the run.'

Effie nodded enthusiastically. 'Like Baz and Ringo?'

Cait smiled wryly. 'If you like.' Baz and Ringo were two cartoon characters in a TV ad for spicy crisps. They wore sombreros and chased around in deserts. Mam never bought the crisps, but Effie was all the time copying their funny accents.

'Bags be Ringo.'

'OK, then I'll be Baz,' said Cait. 'Right, this is the story. We've robbed the bank, got the money in our bags, but we've gotta get across the border before the cops get us.'

'Them low-down dirty cops will be watching us,' Effie feigned an American accent.

'So we're going to hide in this 'ere pick-up, and smuggle ourselves across the border.'

'Will we get away?'

'We'll have to lie real quiet – not make a sound. Comprendez, amigo?'

'You betcha.'

Cait took a last cautious look around. The two men had gone. They must have gone back inside. And with a camper van parked in the way, the girls couldn't be seen from the bus depot either. She prised another loop off its hook and lifted the tarpaulin up as much as she dared.

'OK, Ringo. In you go.'

Climbing up on the vehicle's wheel, Effie slithered eel-like into the darkness. 'Pass me the bags, Baz,' she squeaked.

Cait threw in the bags, then, head-first, squeezed herself under the cover. She was bigger than Effie and the gap was barely wide enough, but by wriggling and heaving, hoping that no one could see her legs flailing around, she managed to get herself in. Putting the bags behind them, she lay down next to her sister. It wasn't too uncomfortable lying on their backs, looking up at the dark blue tarpaulin, but it was very warm.

'It's a hot summer night,' she suggested.

'There ain't no stars,' Effie remarked.

'It's night-time under the clouds then.'

'Time we went to sleep, pardner.'

'Yep. Guess so.'

Effie closed her eyes. 'I'm asleep so. Are you?'

'Me too,' Cait echoed.

They lay in silence for several minutes until a gentle shudder and the sound of an engine starting up caused them suddenly to hold hands.

'Don't make a sound,' Cait instructed.

From out of the corner of her eye, Cait noticed the slight movement as Effie nodded, as best she could, from her lying position. The girls barely breathed as the van backed out and drove away from the station. It stopped on the slip road until there was a break in the traffic, then in too high a gear, it bounded forward.

'Kangaroo petrol,' Cait whispered.

'Shh.' Effie smiled. 'Go to sleep, Baz.'

'OK, Ringo.' Cait was grinning. This really was an adventure.

The van lurched and Effie rolled over towards Cait. 'That's a corner,' she said.

Cait rolled towards Effie. Slowly. 'And that's a roundabout.'

'And another corner.' Effie rolled.

'There's another.'

'A corner again.'

'And again.'

'And yet another corner.'

'Whoops. That's a big roundabout.'

After that there were fewer twists and turns and Cait reckoned they must be on a main road. There would be nothing around but other traffic. She relaxed a little, folding her hands across her stomach and crossing her legs at the ankles.

'There's a star out now, Ringo.'

'Where? Where's the star, Baz?'

'Over there.' Cait moved one finger.

'The clouds must have shifted.' Effie grunted in her bad-guy voice. 'Be a good day tomorrow.'

'Star light. Star bright. First star I see tonight.'

'Baz.'

'Yeah, Ringo.'

'Mexican bandits don't wish on stars.'

'Don't they?'

'Nope.'

'Why not?'

'They just don't.' Effie squinted over at her sister. 'What were you going to wish for anyways?'

'Dunno. Just wishing, I suppose.'

They rode in silence for some time. Cait let herself become mesmerised by the shadows that flickered over their tarpaulin cover, and the sounds that accompanied them. There was the heavy growl of an articulated lorry and the blackness as it passed them by. The soundlessness of the trees and the slight movements of their soft shadows as their leaves moved. And the short swoop and darting shadow as they passed under a bridge. She let the sounds and the shapes wash over her, like the waves had when, sitting on the hard, flat sand at Spit Beach, she'd let the tide's ripples climb up her legs.

'Cait?' Effie broke the silence.

'What is it, Ringo?'

'Cait.' Effie's voice was very small. Sort of brittle and wobbly. 'Can we not be Baz and Ringo? Not just for a minute?'

'OK,' Cait spoke softly as she reached out for her sister's hand. 'You OK?'

'Mmmm.' Effie was about to speak. Cait knew. She waited. 'Cait.' Effie tried again. 'Do you suppose Mam and Dad are up there?'

'Where?'

'Up there with our star. In heaven.'

Cait squeezed Effie's fingers lightly. 'Of course they are.'

'But Dad did a bad thing, didn't he? And when you do a bad thing you don't go to heaven. Do you?'

'Well, maybe not if you're really bad.'

'Was Dad really bad?'

'No. Of course not. He was our Dad, wasn't he?'

'But he's dead. And so's Mam.'

'Yes.' Cait's voice was very small. She did not want to admit the fact.

'So he must have been bad.'

'I don't think he meant to.' Cait was reassuring. 'I think it was an accident.'

'An accident?'

'Yes. An accident. And they can't keep you out of heaven for doing something that's an accident.'

'Can't they?'

'No.' Cait made herself sound positive.

'That's all right then.' Effie sounded happier. 'Goodnight, Baz.'

'Goodnight, Ringo.'

'And, Baz …

'What now?'

43

'That's not a star, anyways.'

'It's not?'

'No. It's just a little hole in the tarpaulin. Look, I can stick my finger in it.'

Effie stuck her finger in the hole, shutting off the pin-prick of light. Cait leaned over, grabbing her arm and pinning it down against a roll of material. 'Don't! If somebody saw your finger!'

'They'd think it was a maggot,' Effie giggled, flexing her finger. 'A wriggling little maggot.'

'Ah stop,' Cait said. 'You're making me laugh.'

The van suddenly veered to the side. They could hear the click of its indicator.

'Where are we going?'

'We must be off the motorway.'

'How do you know?'

'The ground sounds different. It's more crunchy. Not so smooth.'

'Do you think we're in Bristol already?'

'I don't know.'

The van drove over gravel and came to a halt. They heard the 'gnuck' as the handbrake went on and the loud 'clunk' following the 'click' as the door was opened and shut.

'What do we do now?' Effie whispered.

'I don't know,' Cait said. 'I'll try and look out.'

'I want to go to the toilet, anyways,' said Effie.

chapter four

Cait peeped out cautiously. Although the day was still fine, the outside air felt considerably cooler, like wind blowing in at an open window when you're tucked up in bed. The van had stopped in a car park. It was a pub car park, Cait knew. She'd waited in enough pub car parks to know how they looked.

'Where are we?' Effie was excitedly nudging at her bottom.

'I don't know yet.'

'What can you see? Tell me,' the small voice behind her implored.

'Cars mostly. On account of us being in a car park. Some vans and a bus.'

'A bus!'

Cait laughed to herself, looking at the brightly coloured vehicle at the far end of the car park. It might have the shape of a bus, but there the resemblance ended. For a start it was painted a sort of jungly orange and green, with tigers and lions roaming around on its sides.

'Wrong sort of bus,' Cait said as she flopped back into the heat beside her sister. 'We may as well stay here.'

'But I need to do a pee,' Effie insisted, clambering over her sister and squeezing out through the gap. Dismayed, Cait had no option but to follow, dragging their bags out with her.

The back entrance to the pub was at the end of a short path between two newly planted flower-beds. A low green door was set back in rough brickwork. Pubs always made Cait nervous; full of men with beer-breath and sad eyes. She tried to steer Effie away.

'Why don't you go over there? Behind the bushes.' She pointed to the mounds of yellow gorse that bordered the car park.

'Someone might see me,' Effie whined. 'I want a proper toilet.'

'OK,' Cait conceded, pushing open the green door beneath the sign, which said, in fancy writing, 'Jamaica Inn'. The toilets were just inside. Just as if the pub owners were expecting people in the car park to want to go to the toilet, but didn't want them to go behind the bushes, so they put the toilets in a handy place, just inside the back door. After she had finished, Effie carefully washed her hands. 'Where are we, anyways?' she asked.

'I dunno.' Then as the idea suddenly struck her, Cait reached for her bag. 'Hang on, we'll have a look.' Taking out the map, she spread it across the sink. Together they scanned over the place names west of Bristol. 'I don't even know what we're looking for.' Cait eventually folded the map up in disgust. 'Jamaica Inn's the name of the pub, not a place.'

'We'll ask someone.'

'Oh yeah,' Cait sneered. 'Excuse me, but where are we?

That would really sound smart.'

Effie flushed. She hated it when her sister used that tone of voice to her.

Cait picked up on her discomfort straight away. 'I'm sorry. I didn't mean it like that. Come on, I'll buy you something nice.' She led her sister out into the corridor.

'You wouldn't be allowed,' Effie protested, peering round an open door into the bar. 'This is a pub.'

'We could go in there,' Cait indicated another door. 'That says Family Room.'

'Yeah, but we're not a family.' Effie's lip was still up.

'We'll pretend we are,' Cait bent over and kissed the top of her head. 'Me and you and Mi Mi. Our own little family.'

Effie remained unconvinced. 'Let's go back to the van.'

'Would you rather that?'

Effie nodded.

They had to stand back as a group of people with a dog on a rope pushed through the back door. Only the dog took a second glance at the two girls, sniffing at Effie's ear until its owner tugged it on. Outside there was a slight breeze. The heat of the day had passed. Cait reckoned it was sometime in the late afternoon. They walked back along the row of cars, all the way to the end.

'Where is it?' Cait was confused.

'It *was* here.'

'Well, it's not here now.'

'It's gone.' Effie stood, palms turned outwards, her expression hopeless.

'Blast.'

'What are we going to do now?'

'I don't know.'

In spite of the 'leave me alone' tone in her sister's voice,

Effie sidled up close. 'I think you'd better buy me something nice after all,' she said. 'I need to be cheered up.'

They went into the Family Room, where there were lots of resin-scented fishing nets and plastic lobsters, and a counter where you could buy food. It was mostly of the pasty and chip variety, but Effie decided they really needed an ice cream. She got one that was covered in red stuff and knobbly bits, while Cait picked a choc-ice. At the other end of the room, French doors opened on to a garden. In the patio area there were tables and parasols, beyond that, a children's play area. Cait and Effie strolled down and sat on the two swings. Concentrating on her ice cream and listening to the creak of the rope, as she swayed gently, Cait tried to think of nice things.

She tried to imagine what it would be like if this was only the first day of their summer holidays and they would soon be going to Nana and Granda's. The way it used to be. If she listened hard enough, she could even hear Dad whistling as he packed the car with all their things. He had a lovely summery sort of whistle, making up tunes as he went along. Try as she might, Cait had never managed to whistle like him. She used to try, pursing her lips together like a hen's bum, but the most she could manage was a sort of breathy hiss, like air coming out of an air-bed.

'Old granny's whistle,' Dad used to laugh, clapping her on the back for trying. It wasn't fair; Effie could whistle and she was only half her age. She could do Dad's favourite, the one he called 'The Furry Dance', as well as a passable impression of 'The Fields of Athenry'. Then with two fingers in her mouth she could make a piercing shriek, almost as loud as Dad's. Mam used to give out to Dad like mad for encouraging her.

'It's not the done thing for a girl. You'll make her sound like a corner-boy.'

And Effie would look up at her and smile, showing her mouth mixture of adult teeth and baby pearls, and anything less like a corner-boy you would never see. But Mam was very particular about the 'done thing'. She'd nearly given up on Cait, but she liked Effie to wear dresses and put glitter bobbles in her hair. Dad said what did it matter what she wore, but Mam said it did and she would, so she did.

When they were going to Nana's they'd leave on a Saturday. Dad would stay one night and go home Sunday, so he'd be back for work on Monday. Mam would usually stay a week, but then she had to go back to work as well. Nana used to hug her when she was going. She didn't hug Dad, although Granda might sort of shake his hand quickly, as he mumbled, 'Good luck now.' Nana would be kind of quiet the rest of the day after Mam went back, but by the following morning she'd be singing in the kitchen again and bringing the girls down to feed the ducks on the pond behind their house. She and Effie would stay there for most of the summer, until Dad would come for them again in time to get their books and clothes for school. A thought struck Cait. What would happen this year? Would they have to go to a new school? Who'd buy them books this time? She'd be going up to secondary school, but Effie liked their old school. She liked her teacher. It wouldn't be fair, Cait thought, to make her go someplace else. Before Effie started, Cait had already changed schools twice. She hated that. She hated always being the new girl, when everyone else already had their friends picked. She'd just be getting used to a school, when something would happen and Dad would take her out. He'd refuse to send her back until the social workers got her a place in a different one. Each time he'd say it was because there was a 'bad element', and he wouldn't have his daughter exposed to a bad element. Cait had often wondered what he'd meant. She knew there was an element in a kettle, because theirs was always breaking – but she didn't think that was what Dad meant. She licked the last of her ice cream, staring far away at the mounds of gorse up on the hillside and quietly humming the tune her father had whistled.

'Hey! That's our swing.'

Cait snapped out of her thoughts. A scruffy-looking boy of about twelve, wearing battered sandals, was scowling at her. Behind him were a couple of smaller children, barefoot and wearing huge T-shirts down to their knees. On account of their long hair, Cait assumed them to be girls.

'Do you hear me?' the boy's tone was aggressive. 'This is *our* place. Mine and me brothers.'

Cait's initial thought was, 'Oh, so they're not girls then,' but she was tired and worried, so she simply stared at him.

'You deaf? Or stupid? I said …'

'That you own this place?' Cait was smugly sarcastic as she gave a cursory look around. 'Don't see anyone's names on it.'

'Well, are you getting off, or not?'

'No.'

The boy was stunned for a moment. He was obviously not used to being refused. 'Well, there's three of us and only two of you.'

Cait glanced to her side. Effie was still sitting on the other swing. She was pleased to see she hadn't moved either. 'So?'

'So, you're outnumbered.'

'Big deal.'

'Listen, girl,' the boy was obviously annoyed; he was waving two hands at her. 'I don't think you know who you're dealing with here.'

'Nor do I care.'

'I'm Storm Templar. And these are my brothers Deo and Rebus.'

'Pleased to meet you, Storm,' Cait was smilingly polite. 'I'm Cait and this is my sister Effie.'

Rebus gave a sort of snorting laugh. 'Effie! What sort of a name's that?'

Effie heard the jibe and, leaning forward, stuck her tongue out. Hard.

'Effie, that's rude.'

Cait immediately wished she hadn't said anything. Her reprimand had just come out, like it was automatic, like it was something Mam would say. Now the three boys were mimicking her accent, repeating 'Oh Effie, that's rude,' over and over.

'It takes little to amuse you. That's for sure.'

Storm Templar stood with his hands in the pockets of his shorts, staring at her. Cait stared back. She had nothing to lose. He wasn't a bad-looking boy, she considered. From what she could see, at any rate. Through the dirt on his face, she could just make out the freckles over his nose. She had freckles like that, too. 'A little army,' Mam would say. 'Marching from one cheek to the other.'

'You on holiday?' Storm challenged.

'No.' This was true, thought Cait. On holiday you were happy. She wasn't happy. 'Are you?' she demanded.

'No.'

Nil all, thought Cait. 'Do you live round here?'

'For the moment,' Storm replied. '*You* don't.'

'How do you know I don't?'

'Haven't seen you round here before.'

Cait was annoyed at his presumption, but said nothing. She noticed that his brothers, Deo and Rebus, had wandered off to dig in the sandpit. Effie had got down from the swing and was standing watching them in silent curiosity. It was just her and this scruffy boy. Without his brothers behind him, Storm acted less aggressively. He ambled over to the vacant swing.

'Hey!' Cait stopped him. 'That's Effie's swing.'

Storm hesitated, looked back at Cait from under his unruly fringe. 'Don't see her name on it,' he smiled, as he sat firmly on the seat.

For a while the pair of them sat in silence, their arms wrapped around the swing ropes, their toes brushing the ground as they swayed rather than swung, both of them looking vacantly back up at the pub.

'Did you ever see the ghost?'

Cait looked at him. 'What ghost?'

'Rebus says he saw it,' Storm went on. 'It walks through the pub most nights. Right through. On account this used to be a place where smugglers met and stashed their loot. They say the ghost is one of them. They were always quarrelling and fighting in them times. Getting themselves killed an' that.'

'And he comes here every night?' Cait felt a shudder start at the base of her spine and work its way up. Wherever else she and Effie spent the night, she hoped it wouldn't be around here.

'Do you believe in ghosts?' Storm asked her. 'That the dead can come back?'

Cait said nothing. The dead were not something she wanted to think about right now.

'You know,' Storm persisted. 'If someone dies in bad circumstances, their soul can't rest. Then they wander the earth as a ghost.'

Cait was suddenly afraid – and angry. 'Would you ever shut up about your stupid ghosts. If you've nothing better to say, you can just bog off.'

Storm shut up like he'd been stung. Girls didn't usually tell him to get lost like that, like they really meant it. He swayed a bit more in silence to indicate that he'd got the message, then in a quiet voice asked, 'Well, if you're not on holiday, and you're not from around here – and I know you're not 'cause otherwise you would have known about, you know – what are you doing here?'

Cait surprisingly thought about Baz and Ringo. What would they do? This lad didn't look like he'd grass on them. Would *Baz* tell the truth? He would.

'We're on the run.'

'Get away.' Storm looked at her as if he knew he was being fooled.

'Are, so.'

'Don't believe you.'

It was obvious to Cait that Storm's imagination was not on a level with hers. Mind you, she reckoned, if she really did tell him the truth, he definitely wouldn't believe her. Either she should say nothing, or make up something more plausible.

'We *are*,' she insisted. 'We're running away.'

'What from?' Storm was still in 'you're kidding me' mode.

'From the Home. We're orphans, see.' At least *that* bit, Cait thought, was true. 'The police are after us.' Well, they probably would be soon, she reckoned.

Storm's jaw had dropped visibly, Cait noticed, and

knew she was on a roll. 'We couldn't stay in the Home. They were awful to us. Really awful. Mean and cruel. They used to beat us and lock us in cupboards and everything. So we ran away.'

Storm was now wide-eyed, impressed. 'Wow.'

Cait suddenly had an idea. 'Effie,' she called, 'come here to me.' Obediently Effie came over and Cait showed Storm her legs, pointing out the bruises from where she fell on the rocks. 'See that,' she said. 'See where they beat her? I wouldn't let no one beat my sister like that. Would you?'

Glancing over at his brothers, Storm shook his head vigorously. 'No way,' was his emphatic answer.

Cait was pleased. They had an ally at last.

'Will you go to London?' Storm asked the question innocently, as if in the belief that everyone running away somehow ended up in London.

'London? Why London?'

Storm shrugged.

'Are you mad?' Cait turned away, indicating quite clearly that she didn't want to be questioned any more on the subject.

'Kids!' A woman's voice roared out from the top of the garden. Three tousled heads, two in the sandpit and one on the swing, jerked up towards the patio.

'Meet you back on the bus!' Storm shouted.

'OK.'

Cait glanced up just in time to catch a glimpse of a floaty, multi-coloured skirt swish back through the French windows. Sliding from his seat, Storm began rounding up his brothers and reminded Cait suddenly of a sheep-dog. Sand still clinging to their knees, Storm had Deo and Rebus under reluctant control.

'Come with us.'

Cait hesitated.

'Or have you a better idea?'

The brief thought of the rampaging ghost was enough to make up her mind. She called Effie, quickly checked they both had their bags, and followed the boys as they disappeared into the overgrown shrubbery that bordered the garden. Ducking under low branches, wading over brambles, they eventually squeezed, by way of a broken slat, out through the wooden fence and into the car park. Grabbing Effie by the hand, Cait ran after Storm and his brothers, simultaneously noting in some awe that Deo and Rebus had been running over the prickly grass and spiky gravel – in their bare feet. They stopped beside the jungly painted bus.

'This?'

Storm grinned at Cait. 'Like it?' Without waiting for an answer, he opened the door. 'Come in, then.'

'It's not locked?'

'Who'd steal it,' Storm laughed, 'and get away with it?'

It was the girls' turn to be impressed. The inside of the bus was like no bus they had ever seen before. For a start there were no rows of seats, two by two with an aisle running up the middle. The only seats they could see were two benches, lengthways to the windows, just inside the door. There was a table in front of one, and beside the other, some of the windows had been blanked out and cupboards, a cooker and a sink put in. It reminded Cait of the inside of a caravan.

'Quick! In here.'

Cait had scarcely noticed the heavy curtain blocking off the back part of the bus, until she was dragged through it by Storm.

'Daisy and me old man will be back in a minute.'

'Will they mind us being here?'

'I'll have to talk to them first.'

'How old?' Effie was tugging at Storm's T-shirt. She wasn't being shy, Cait noticed. She must like him.

'Me?'

'This old man,' Effie explained. 'Is he your granda?'

'Who? Jason? No. He's me dad. Well, he's not my *real* dad, but he's my dad. You know.'

'Is Daisy your mother, then?' Cait enquired.

'Yeah.'

'Why do you call her Daisy,' Effie asked.

''Cause it's her name.'

'Oh.' Cait said nothing more. Her mam's name was Joan, but they never called her that. They only ever called her Mam. Mam and Dad. The sound of voices outside suddenly startled her.

'They're coming!' Storm hissed. 'Get in there and keep quiet.' He pushed them – gently – onto the bottom bunk of two beds that were fixed to the wall of the bus. There were two more on the opposite side. An old grey blanket hung down from the top bunk and they crept behind that.

'That's Rebus's den,' Storm told them. 'But he won't mind.'

Cait and Effie tucked their legs up in the furthest corner of Rebus's bed, wrapped their arms around their knees and waited.

'Boys smell,' Effie whispered to her sister, 'don't they?'

A click of the door silenced them. Storm disappeared to the far side of the curtain. They heard voices.

'You here already?' It was a man's voice.

'We came by a short cut.' That was Storm.

'You must be in a hurry to go.' This was a woman's

voice. Cait presumed it to be Daisy, Storm's mam. 'Usually we'd have to drag you lot out of the play area.'

'Yeah, well, it got boring. It's really only for kids.'

'And what are you?' Their dad's voice sounded nice. Sort of young and jokey.

'Well,' said Storm. 'Younger kids.'

'Like babies,' said a younger voice, with scorn. It could have been either Deo or Rebus.

'Lucky we're moving on, then,' the mother said.

'Moving? Where?'

'The others have gone on already. Jason had a bit of business to do in Bodmin this afternoon, so we're catching up with them at Two Bridges this evening.'

'Two Bridges?' It was Storm asking.

'Dartmoor,' their mother said.

'Not far from the prison. So if you're not good …' Their dad must have made a face because Rebus and Deo suddenly squeaked in pretend terror.

Bodmin and Dartmoor. These were important words. Cait repeated them over and over in her head. She would look them up on the map as soon as she got the chance. There was no more talking for a moment. Cait heard footsteps going up the bus – going away from them. She heard a curtain swishing. The footsteps came back.

'I've left stuff there on my bed.' (It was their father.) 'Don't let Deo and Rebus near it. Nor you, neither.'

'OK, OK.'

The door clicked again. Open. 'Now keep the door shut.'

There was a chorus of voices. 'We won't,' they teased.

'And if we're stopped or anything. You know what to do.'

'We don't.'

'See you in Two Bridges then.'

The door slammed shut and Cait let out the breath she hadn't realised she'd been holding. Storm stuck his head around the curtain.

'You OK?'

'Yeah. Fine.' Cait said. 'You didn't tell them?'

'Have to find the right moment.'

'And they won't mind?'

''Course they won't.'

If they were as nice as their voices sounded, Cait thought, he might well be right. She hoped so.

'Where did they go?' Effie enquired.

'To drive the bus.' Storm made it sound as if it were patently obvious. 'You can get to the front from the inside, but you'd have to climb over things. It's easier to walk around the outside.' The vehicle suddenly shuddered and Storm instinctively put out a hand to steady himself. Cocooned in Rebus's den, on his bunk, behind the heavy curtain, Cait could hear the muffled roar as from somewhere beneath them the engine grumbled into life.

chapter five

When they felt safe enough to sneak out of Rebus's den, Cait spread the map out on the floor. She found Bodmin quite easily, and was disappointed that the lift they took with Evans and Co. had not even brought them out of Cornwall. Dartmoor seemed to refer to a big purplish area on the map. There were not many roads crossing it, so Cait presumed it would be wild and hilly like the Burren, near where Nana and Granda lived. It was in Devon, the county next to Cornwall, but still the wrong side of Bristol.

'Whatcha doing?' Storm's head suddenly poked around the curtain.

Cait rapidly folded the map. 'Nothing.'

'Can I come in?'

Cait shrugged. 'It's your place.'

Storm joined them on their side of the curtain. 'I've left Deo and Rebus doing some colouring. That'll keep them busy for a while. Well, five minutes maybe.' He stuck his head back through the curtain. 'And don't go near Dad's stuff, neither.'

Neither child answered verbally, although Cait well-imagined the faces they would probably be making. Effie would, if she spoke to her like that. Storm sat cross-legged on the floor, picking at a scab on his knee. Cait had a head full of questions, but didn't know what would be pertinent to ask.

'Are your parents Travellers?' she asked as innocently as she could.

'Travellers?' Storm didn't understand the significance of the word.

'You know. Travellers.' Cait hesitated to say "gypsies" or something more derogatory. 'I mean – is this bus your home?'

Storm laughed, understanding what she was getting at. 'It's home for the summer. Rest of the year we live in an ordinary house.'

'Sort of "part-time" Travellers?' Cait suggested.

Storm shifted his position slightly. 'Mum … Daisy and Jason say "travelling is a state of mind,"' then aware of Cait's faintly bemused expression, he added, 'whatever that means.'

Cait changed the subject. 'I like your bus.'

Effie nudged her, her eyebrows lowered. 'It smells funny.'

'Well, it's not really our bus,' Storm admitted. 'It belongs to my uncle.'

'Is he a Traveller, then?' Effie asked.

'He does travel a lot,' Storm said. 'But he lets us have it in the summer. Nice way to spend the holidays.'

'We go to New Quay for our holidays,' Effie said. 'We go to see …' but a quick elbow from Cait silenced her from saying any more.

'We were in Newquay last week,' Storm jumped at what

he thought was a common interest.

Effie's eyes widened, but Cait quashed her sister's wondering. 'He means Newquay in Cornwall.'

Just before Storm could ask what other Newquay she could mean, Deo pushed his head through the curtain. 'How long till we get there?'

'A little while,' Storm answered. 'Go back to your colouring.'

But Deo didn't feel like colouring. He sat down crosslegged next to Storm, watching Effie and Cait in silent curiosity. Pretty soon Rebus came to join them, saying that it was boring being out on his own. To pass the time they played 'I spy' until Storm and Rebus fell into an argument about whether or not the word 'ceiling' began with an 's'. Effie had quickly lost interest in the game, and had fallen asleep, her head resting against her sister's shoulder. Cait stared vacantly out of the back window at the puffy clouds racing away behind them, while Storm and his brothers called an uneasy truce. Eventually the bus turned off the main road, and twisting and turning, travelled down a series of roads that Cait could see from her rear view were getting progressively narrower and more overgrown. She listened nervously to the sound of leaves and branches scraping along the roof, as she braced herself against the bumpy movement of the bus, so as not to disturb her sister. Effie woke up anyhow, and looked around, startled as the bus suddenly came to a halt. With the engine turned off, Cait was amazed at how quiet it had become.

'They'll be coming in now,' Storm said urgently. 'Hide in Rebus's den.'

As Cait crawled in behind the blanket, dragging Effie with her, the boys went back out through the curtain, just as the door clicked open.

'OK, kids. We're here. Everybody out.'

Deo and Rebus shot out like sheep through a gap, but Storm hung back, making out he'd forgotten something, until his parents, arm in arm, had turned and strolled away from the bus.

'Coast is clear,' Storm hissed. 'Quick now.'

Taking cautious glances about them, Cait and Effie crept from their hiding place and out of the bus.

'When are you going to tell your parents about us?' Cait asked.

'Don't worry,' Storm reassured her. 'I have a plan.'

Outside, the day was beginning to darken, and Cait was glad they had brought their jackets. They had stopped in a sort of rough car park. It wasn't a car park with tarmac, walls and gates, but rather a flattish piece of ground where there was more earth and rocks showing than grass. There were a few other vehicles here already. One or two caravans, several campers and one other painted bus.

'It's like a dream,' remarked Effie, in awe.

She was right, thought Cait. The other bus was painted in shades of blue that got progressively darker towards the wheels. It was decorated with white stars, rainbow-coloured people and fish with wings.

'There's a shark!' said Effie. 'Like the ones we seen.'

Storm snorted. 'That's not a shark. It's a dolphin.'

'Dolphins don't have wings,' Cait adopted a no-nonsense tone she hoped would pay Storm back for ridiculing her sister.

'They're the spirits of dead dolphins.'

Cait wrinkled part of her nose in a kind of 'yeah, what planet are you from' expression, but Effie clapped her hands, smiling.

'Angel dolphins! Dolphin angels.'

A light breeze carrying the scent of something cooking changed the subject and Cait suddenly realised how hungry she was. It had been a long time since the ice cream at the Jamaica Inn, and even longer since their burger and chips outside Woollies.

'Come on, let's eat.'

The girls hung back, but Storm encouraged them. 'Come on. No one will mind. There's so many kids around, no one will even notice you.'

He was right. There seemed to be zillions of them, Cait thought. Most of the adults were sitting around a small bonfire, chatting and eating, but the children were all over the place. Darting about, playing games and all dressed like Deo and Rebus in huge T-shirts and not much else. Around the far side of one of the caravans, a gas stove had been set up. A woman in a brightly coloured headscarf was ladling some sort of a stew out of a huge black pot. Daisy and Jason, Storm's parents, were holding out bowls to be filled.

'Sorry we couldn't wait for you,' the headscarf woman was saying. 'The kids said they were starving. We nearly had a mutiny.'

Daisy laughed good-naturedly, looking over at Rebus and Deo, sitting on two stones, already shovelling huge spoonfuls of stew into their mouths.

'Here,' said Storm. 'Grab a bowl.'

The girls held out their bowls to be filled and the headscarf woman smiled. 'Come back when you've finished. There's plenty more.'

'What is it?' hissed Effie to Cait, as they perched on two rocks near the fire.

Cait prodded her stew with her spoon. It was grey and kind of lumpy, but it smelled good.

'It's magic stew,' she whispered to Effie. 'It'll give you good dreams.'

Effie looked doubtfully at the congealing mess in her bowl, but when a sideways glance told her that Cait was already eating, she dug in her spoon and began. She ate gingerly at first, but then with increasing gusto, until there was nothing left in her bowl but one half of a haricot bean.

'That's just what Ringo would have liked.' Effie licked her lips with satisfaction.

'Is he back now?' asked Cait.

'Nah.' Effie stretched out her legs, crossing her ankles as she surveyed all around her. 'But he would have liked it if he was.'

Cait put down her empty bowl. Her tummy felt uncomfortable. Could hardly be the beans already, could it? she thought. She sat it out for as long as she could, but eventually was forced to go over to Storm, and whisper in his ear.

'Is there a toilet on your bus. I have to go.'

Storm shook his head. His mouth was full. He was already on his second bowlful. Cait must have looked horrified – as well as desperate – for he wiped his mouth and pointed to a black bucket, some distance away, near a little path leading into a wooded area.

'I'm not going in a bucket!' Cait was highly insulted. Storm gave a spluttering laugh.

'It's not funny.' Cait was indignant.

'No, but you are,' said Storm, as he swallowed his last mouthful. 'No, you go into the woods. There's loo paper in the bucket. And a trowel.'

'A trowel?'

'Dig a hole first and bury it after,' Storm explained.

Cait said no more. Be brave, she thought to herself.

Pretend you do this sort of thing every day of the week. Go to the bathroom in the middle of nowhere, surrounded by a whole pile of strangers. Mind you, if it was bad for her, it'd be even worse for Effie. She wouldn't even go behind a bush at Jamaica Inn, when there was no one around. She'd better take her along though. Call her over. Walk nonchalantly to the bucket and off into the woods. No one would notice.

'Effie,' she called. 'Come here a minute.'

The two girls strolled down towards the black bucket. Sure enough, there was the toilet paper and the trowel. Effie gave her a funny look, but followed her sister down the path into the woods.

'Hey kids!' A voice suddenly stopped them dead. 'Make sure you don't pee in the river. We need the water to wash.'

Cait felt the colour rise in her cheeks. Never had she been so embarrassed. She couldn't turn round. She had probably gone redder than the bonfire by now, she reckoned. Why did that stupid person have to call out? Slowly, annoyance took over. Mexican bandits wouldn't feel like this, she was sure. They'd just go and wouldn't give a … She took a deep breath. Here goes, she thought, taking a few steps forward again. 'Come on, Ringo, partner,' she said. 'Baz is here again.'

Rebus and Deo were already in bed when Cait, Storm and Effie went back to the bus. They had been sitting round the fire with the adults and some of the older children. Someone was playing a guitar. Effie had fallen asleep again and Cait sat with her arms around her, wondering how it was that yesterday seemed such a long time ago. Eventually, after standing up and yawning, Storm beckoned them over to the bus with him. Effie grumbled a bit at being woken, but allowed herself to be guided into the vehicle.

'You can sleep in the bunk under mine, if you like.'

'Did you tell your parents about us?' Cait asked sleepily.

Storm was about to say something, but the sound of footsteps outside stopped him. Daisy came in.

'Time for bed,' she said to Storm, while raising an eyebrow quizzically in the direction of Cait and Effie.

'Is it OK,' Storm said, 'if Lin and Eva stay?'

Daisy raised the eyebrow higher – questioning.

'They're Charmain's sister's kids. But there's a drip coming in on them in their caravan.'

'Well …'

'I asked Charmain's sister and she said it was OK.'

'It'll be a bit of a squash …'

'They don't mind. Do you, Lin?' Storm kicked Cait under the table.

'No, that's fine,' Cait found herself replying.

Daisy started with recognition. 'Isn't that an *Irish* accent?'

Cait was suddenly flummoxed. She didn't know she *had* an accent.

'Charmain doesn't have an Irish sister.' Daisy queried.

'Lin's dad is.' Storm answered with authority.

Daisy looked hard at her son, but Cait noticed he didn't flinch. 'Well, OK then. But it's still bedtime for you kids.'

The three children sat looking at her. Well, two of them anyway. Effie was yawning.

'Well, get gone then,' Daisy insisted. 'I'll be back in a few minutes.'

As the children disappeared behind the curtain, with Cait dragging the sleepy Effie, and the door clicked shut, Cait rounded on Storm.

'So, I'm Lin, am I?'

'First name I could think of.' Storm held up his hands apologetically. 'You didn't want me to use your real names did you? Not if the police are after you?'

'Suppose not.' Cait began rearranging the blanket on the lower bunk. 'Anyway, who's Chairmain's sister?'

Storm shrugged. 'Haven't a clue. First thing I could think of.'

'Thanks, anyway.' Having an imaginary mother, Cait told herself, was perhaps better than no mother at all. She rolled Effie over to the wall side of the bunk, fished Mi Mi out of the 'My Little Pony' rucksack and tucked it in beside her in case she would be looking for it in the night.

Storm kicked off his sandals and scrambled up to the top bunk. 'G'night, then. See you in the morning.'

''Night,' Cait replied.

Lying awake, surrounded by snores and night-time snuffles of sleeping children, Cait heard Daisy and Jason finally come back. She kept her eyes shut when she heard them come over, draw back the curtain and peep in at them all.

'Didn't know Charmain had a sister,' Jason was saying.

'Well, we're not doing anything about that now,' Daisy replied. 'Wait till the morning.'

Jason snorted. 'Didn't I tell you when you let him keep that puppy he'd found and brought home, that he'd be forever picking up waifs and strays.'

'But these are children,' his wife insisted. 'Not waifs and strays. Innocent little children.'

'Don't I know that,' Jason said wryly. 'They may be innocent, but mark my words, they'll be bringing trouble with them.'

'Come on, Jay,' Daisy whispered, and from the muffled

tone of her voice, Cait guessed she was kissing him or something disgusting like that. 'We'll talk in the morning.'

With a breath of relief, Cait realised they were gone, and she snuggled in closer to Effie. She slept fitfully, being awakened by dreams that seemed full of dolphin spirits flying on feathery wings. Above them, sharks wearing black uniforms swam around with guns. In rows on their fins glinted the bright silver buttons of the police force.

chapter six

The low sun of a blue-skied morning spread warmth across their blanket and Cait woke, blinking sleep-filled eyes and stretching the stiffness out of her legs. Effie was nestled in beside her, curled like a sleeping kitten. With spread fingers, Cait ran her hand gently through her sister's hair, combing it.

Effie woke suddenly. 'Where are we?'

Cait kissed the top of her head, the way Mam used to do. 'Safe,' she whispered. 'Lie quiet.'

Effie rolled on to her back and Cait made room. Her eyes were wide open, blue and bright as marbles as she stared upwards, but at least she wasn't crying. Cait turned towards the window, shutting her own eyes from the brightness of the sun. Somewhere, birds were singing and, like wind in a reed bed, the soft 'whhoo-oop' of a wood pigeon. It would be just like this, she thought, if they were in Nana's, where they'd be lying in the wooden bed Granda had made for them in the little attic bedroom with walls that sloped down to the floor – and they'd be lying awake,

69

wondering what they'd do when the day really began. She imagined she could hear the clank of Granda's pail from when he'd come in from milking the goat, and the sounds of Nana in the kitchen scolding the cats for jumping up on the presses. She always loved that little room. Granda had done it up especially for her and Effie when they got too big to share their mother's room downstairs. It had been the loft, 'a waste of space', Granda had called it, in his usual gruff way, 'good for nothing but breeding dust and cobwebs'. Nana said it'd be too cold in the winter, but in the summer, when they came, with the sun heating up the tiles of the roof above them, it was grand.

Somewhere in the distance she could hear voices – children's voices. That'd be the Naughton kids from next door, she told herself. Going down to the beach early – just like they always did – to see what the sea had brought in. The Naughtons were just about the only children Cait and Effie played with – and that was only because there was no one else. With all the schools she'd been to, Cait had had little time to make any real friends. In any case, she was never allowed to bring anyone home. Mam explained it was because she'd be at work and Dad always said wasn't it enough that they had each other? Most times it was. Others of her age might have made fun of her if they knew she played make-believe games with a six-year-old, but Effie liked playing 'pretends' and, Cait thought, if she was really truthful with herself, so did she. Under the blanket, her hand had found Effie's. She squeezed it gently, just as she would waking up in Nana's house. Then a sudden noise startled her, her eyes flashed open and the dream was gone. Storm had jumped from the top bunk and was beside them.

'I'm starving,' he announced. 'Anyone want breakfast?'

Breakfast was cornflakes out of a jumbo-sized packet poured into chipped white china bowls. Storm ate his standing up because he said there was no room on the bench at the table. Cait was relieved that Jason was nowhere to be seen, and Daisy said nothing more awkward to her than to ask how she'd slept.

Scraping the last flake from his dish, Rebus wiped his milk moustache with the dirty hem of his long T-shirt. 'Can we go now?'

As Deo followed his brother out, Cait and Effie slid off the bench behind them. Firing his spoon into the sink, Storm drank noisily at the milk from his upturned bowl.

'Mind the girls!' Daisy called out to her youngest sons as Effie jumped down from the bus. 'Not you.' She caught Storm by the arm, just as Cait went out after her sister. 'I want a word with you.'

As the door shut, with Storm still inside and the younger boys running off, chasing each other, Cait and Effie felt suddenly lost.

'What'll we do?' Effie asked.

'If we were at Nana's,' Cait said dreamily. 'We'd go to the beach.'

'With the smelly Naughtons?' Effie wrinkled her nose.

'They're not smelly,' Cait retorted. 'Anyway, I thought you liked Tom.'

'Tom's funny,' Effie admitted. 'But they *do* smell. They smell cabbagy.'

'Nana says that's because their mam never opens the windows.'

There were worse things to smell like, thought Cait, as they stood in the shadow of a gnarled thorn tree that grew nearly out of a rock in the middle of the car park. All about them people moved around the vans, campers and the two buses: washing clothes or cutlery in plastic buckets; hanging stuff on string lines or playing with the dogs that seemed to skulk around, always looking for scraps. One woman was feeding a baby. Holding the infant in the crook of one arm, with her hand spread out across its back, she had its head stuffed up under her blouse. With her other hand she was cutting some man's hair. She was singing as well – a lilting rhythm – but Cait couldn't catch the words. She looked so relaxed and casual, Cait wondered how she managed not to drop the baby, the scissors or the song.

'Come and catch fish!' Rebus had suddenly bounced out in front of them.

'Where?'

'At the river. All the other kids are catching them. There's millions!'

Down at the river with Rebus, Deo, and some of the other children, Cait and Effie tried to catch the tiny black fish that darted about in the warmth of the shallows.

'I wish we had our net,' sighed Effie, as yet again she swiped her hand through the water, uncurled her fist and found nothing but the brown stain of a bit of water weed caught between her fingers.

Cait tried the cupped-hand method, but with no better luck. She held her hands flat against the river bed, palms upwards, then gently closed them as she slowly raised her hands beneath a fish.

'It's no good. I can't catch anything.'

Suddenly Rebus shouted out, 'I've got one!' He was jumping around, waving a clenched fist.

'Show us,' demanded Deo.

'Yeah. Show us.'

Scruffy-haired and T-shirted, the kids crowded round, expectant and excited as Rebus uncurled one finger after another.

'That's not a fish,' someone said.

Lying in his palm was a lump of black jelly.

'Ugh,' said Deo.

'It was alive a moment ago,' said Rebus, prodding it with his finger. 'I swear.'

The lump of jelly seemed to stretch and grow longer. One of the older girls shrieked, 'It's a leech!'

'A bloodsucker,' said a boy.

Panicked, Rebus tried to flick the leech off his palm, but it seemed stuck.

'Suck your blood till you're dry,' taunted Deo.

Rebus flapped his hand about ineffectually. 'I'll get you for this!'

'Put your hand in the water,' the older girl advised. 'It'll wash off.'

'That's if it's not sucking his blood already.' Deo was enjoying his brother's discomfort.

Rebus ran back to the shallows, plunging his hands into the water and making waves. Cait was just wondering if it was worth bothering to try to catch fish anymore, when Storm came running over. He was red in the face and looked worried.

'You've to come back to the bus,' he said. 'Mum and Jason want to talk to you.'

Exchanging a nervous look with her sister, the two girls followed Storm back to the jungly bus. Storm's father, Jason, looked cross.

'OK you guys,' he said as soon as they sat down on the long bench opposite the door. 'What's going on here?'

Cait looked at Storm who looked at Effie, who then looked back at Cait.

'Well?' Jason stood with his hands on his hips. There was a big rip on the front of his T-shirt. In spite of her nervousness, Cait couldn't help noticing the fact that his toes, poking out of their sandals, were very dirty and extremely hairy. 'Em ...' she said, more because the others were looking at her than because she had something to say.

'We know Charmain doesn't have a sister who's married to an Irishman.' Storm's mother spoke quietly. She was standing close and kind of stroking Jason's arm, as if he was some sort of animal that needed to be kept calm in case he got suddenly ferocious.

'Well, who are you?' barked Jason. 'Lin, what about you?'

With a start, Cait realised he was speaking to her and she sort of gasped and spluttered. Jason was shaking his head. 'I don't suppose your name is Lin, any more than your sister's is Eva.' He looked straight at Effie, and Effie – now shaking with fear – began to cry. Storm patted her knee. 'Dad, you're scaring her,' he said accusingly.

Jason ran his hands through his hair in exasperation while Daisy stroked and rubbed in her effort to keep him calm. 'I only want the truth,' he was saying. 'Which of you will tell me that?'

Effie looked at Cait and Cait looked at Storm. She didn't want to think about what was true and what was not. Storm swallowed hard. Effie was upset. The interrogation had gone on quite long enough.

'Their names are Cait and Effie.' Storm kicked his heels against the floor. Jason and Daisy turned around and paid attention.

'Cait and Effie,' repeated Daisy. 'And since Charmain's sister's not your mother ...'

'Their real mother's dead,' Storm interrupted.

Cait's gasp was almost audible, but Daisy's face assumed an expression of troubled sympathy.

'She died by an accident,' Effie suddenly piped up. 'Dad too.'

Daisy's bottom lip went kind of wobbly. 'Oh, I am sorry.'

'They're orphans, Mum.' Storm knew he was getting a firm hold of the weak spot in his mother's heart. 'They got nobody.'

Jason was less easily moved. 'Now, now, Storm. Somebody will have been caring for them. There's nobody as has nobody. Someone will need to know.'

Cait jumped, as with a sudden movement, Storm practically threw himself at Jason's feet, wrapping his arms around his legs.

'Dad, please don't tell nobody! They were at an orphanage, but they were so mean to them they ran away. Please, Dad, don't tell. If you do, they'll make 'em go back and that just wouldn't be fair.'

Cait was speechless. Here was the tough boy, who only yesterday was arguing with her to get off the swing, now kneeling on the floor and crying. He was really and truly crying. But the most amazing thing was that this wasn't like a temper tantrum she'd throw if her Dad was that being hard on her, like sending her to bed when there was something she really wanted to see on the television. Storm wasn't even crying for himself. In spite of the fact that before yesterday he never knew she and Effie existed – and if they went tomorrow, his life would still be the same – he was crying for *her*.

Reaching down, Jason prised Storm off his legs. 'What are you talking about?'

'They were at an orphanage, Dad. But they beat them. They used to beat them every day. For no reason. You never beat us like that, Dad. Poor Effie has bruises and cuts all over from when they beat her. I wouldn't let anyone do that to Deo – or Rebus. I'd kill 'em! So they ran away, Dad. So they wouldn't get beaten again. And if you tell anyone, or if the police find them, they'll just take them right back to get beaten all over again.'

Cait watched and listened in stunned horror as her life history reinvented itself. All this stuff about an orphanage. What if she had told Storm the truth?

Jason picked his son up off the floor. He was smiling.

'You don't believe me.'

'If you're telling me the truth,' Jason said, 'then I'll believe you.'

Storm nodded. 'It's what she told me,' he indicated Cait, 'and I believe her.'

Cait kept her fingers tightly crossed in her lap, hoping Jason wouldn't ask her to corroborate.

Then they were let go. Storm's mother gave Cait several yards of toilet paper to clean up Effie's face. They were given a glass of apple juice each and as soon as it was drunk, they were told to get lost, skedaddle, go outside and play. Glancing back ruefully at the closed door, Storm remarked that his parents would now be talking about them.

'That's rude,' said Effie.

'What is?' asked Cait.

'Talking behind people's backs.'

Storm shrugged. 'Don't know about you. But I'd done enough listening.'

'What'll they say about us?' Cait was anxious. 'What'll they do?'

'I don't know,' Storm admitted. 'I don't think Jason will go to the police though. He's not over-fond of the Law.'

'By the way,' Cait said shyly, 'thanks for standing up for us. You were great.'

Storm stopped, twisting his toe in the ground as if he had a stone in his sandal. The skin behind the freckles, Cait noticed, seemed to have gone suddenly red. But the illusion that Storm was in any way embarrassed was short-lived. 'Yeah, I was, wasn't I?' He tossed the fringe back out of his eyes, grinning. 'My Uncle Pete says I should be an actor.' With a quick wink to Cait, he was off, running back over the spiky grass to the river's edge and the other boys.

Cait and Effie walked on together, as far as the cattle grid that separated the car park from the rest of the moor. They peered down through the bars into the darkness.

'Yeuck,' said Cait. 'Look at all the rubbish!'

Effie squatted for a better look.

'Don't put your hand in there!' Cait warned, as Effie's slim arm slipped easily between the bars. 'There'll be rats and rabies and everything down there!'

Effie withdrew her hand, but kept looking. 'Someone had a McDonald's,' she remarked. 'I can see the packet. Do they have McDonald's over here, or is it only in Ireland?'

'I expect it's all over.'

Effie looked up, as if expecting to see a big neon 'M' rising up over the scrubby furze and bracken. 'I'd love a Happy Meal.'

'Mmm,' Cait agreed.

'Why do they call it that?'

'What?'

'Happy.'

'Dunno. Maybe because it makes you feel that way.'

'Does it work?'

'Let's go back to the river,' Cait changed the subject. 'See if they caught any fish.'

But Effie hadn't finished. 'What was all that about an orphanage?'

The sudden question caught Cait by surprise. 'Orphanage?' she said.

'What Storm was talking about.' Effie narrowed her eyes in the sun as she looked at her sister. 'What he said you told him.'

'Oh that.' Cait tried to make out like it was no big deal. 'If I'd told him what had really happened, he wouldn't have understood.'

'Do you, Cait? Do you understand?'

'Nope,' said Cait, chucking a stone into the cattle grid. The hollow 'ding' of metal seemed to ring out loudly, but nobody came over, or told them to be quiet.

chapter seven

'What day is it?'

Cait thought for a moment, counting on her fingers. 'Sunday, I think. Or it could be Monday. Why?'

Effie didn't look up; she was hunting through the low bushes. 'Mam said we'd go to Nana and Granda's when we got home. We should be back in Ireland now.'

Cait sighed to herself. She'd promised Effie she'd take her home. But that was four days ago and they hadn't got very far. They were still only on the edge of Dartmoor. Still only in Devon.

'We should ring Nana,' Effie suggested. 'So she won't be worried. Tell her we'll be coming soon.'

'Effie,' said Cait in mock seriousness. 'Do you see a telephone round here?'

Effie sighed deeply, her arms flopping to her sides in an affectation of helplessness. 'I mean, when we *find* a telephone.'

'There's some good ones here,' Storm called out without looking up, and his two younger brothers, like cygnets responding to their mother's call, began to wade through the bracken and brambles towards him.

Storm had brought them here, to this spot further down the river, beyond the cattle grid. He said he'd found whortles and, intrigued, Cait and Effie went with him. He called them whortleberries, but Cait said her nana called them 'fraochans'. Either way the soft black berries were ripe and tasted sweet. They'd been here about an hour now, hunting for the tiny fruits hidden in the dark green leaves, and with the sun on their backs, and in spite of the bramble scratches and nettle stings they all had, it was really quite pleasant. In fact, thought Cait, it was quite nice staying here with Storm and his family in their funny jungle-painted bus, even without a toilet or television. His mam had been great to them, and even his dad hadn't asked any more questions. All the same, they *had* to get home. She'd promised Effie. She ran her berry-blackened fingers down the front of her shorts, making a double row of purple-blue stripes. Along with the dirt, the grass marks and the blood stains that may or may not have been hers, her clothes were filthy anyway. Mam would have had a fit. She hated to see either of them in anything that wasn't scrupulously clean. Effie looked up out of the bushes, her face clownish with its big juice-purple mouth. Her hair too, normally so well brushed it shone, was messed up and decorated with stickyback and bits of twig. At least she wasn't crying. She'd been crying so much these past days. Not roaring or screaming or anything, but it was as if someone left a tap running in her eyes. No sooner had she wiped them, than they'd start filling and spilling all over again. Just looking at her made Cait want to cry. More than anything she wanted to give in and wallow in the river of her own tears. But she mustn't do that. She mustn't be weak and give in. She'd be no good to Effie if she did that. She must be strong. Then there were the nightmares. At bedtime Effie now refused to close her eyes. She said the magic stew didn't work and that bad things came in her dreams. She said if she didn't sleep, she wouldn't dream and then the bad things wouldn't come. With Cait beside her, she lay awake for as long as she could, crying silently from fear and exhaustion. Come morning, they would both be tired, but at least Effie cat-napped during the day. She'd always been able to do that. Nana used to say she'd sleep on the head of a pin if she had to. When she slept Cait sat and watched her, making sure none of the other children awoke her.

'Here's Melody!' Effie gave a two-handed wave and Cait looked.

Coming along the narrow track, worn grassless by the hoofs of countless sheep, a girl in a bright pink jump-suit, sunglasses and pink plastic shoes. There was no guessing as to Melody's favourite colour. Just before she got to the bit where the path turned boggy, she stopped, waved and shouted something. Realising she was too far away to be heard, she began to pick her way delicately over the wet bits. Balancing on one leg and then the other, she remind-ed Cait of the flamingos in Dublin Zoo. She should tell her that, Cait thought, laughing to herself. Melody would *hate* it. Melody thought she was wonderful. She was get-ting a figure and liked clothes that fitted. Cait had often caught her preening and posing in the still waters of the ox-bow pool on the far side of the wood. Trouble was, Effie thought Melody was wonderful too. She thought she was pretty and clever. Cait reckoned she was neither. OK so she knew about the leech, but if she didn't paint her face she wouldn't be a bit pretty. Effie liked to watch when

Melody did her make-up, squinting into the wing-mirror of one of the cars. She always wore make-up, just like she always wore pink. Effie was thrilled yesterday when Melody drew two love-hearts on her – one on each cheek – with bright pink lipstick. Effie went round with them on all that day until, blackened with flies and dust, Cait took her to the river and made her wash them off. Yes, Effie thought Melody was wonderful. Cait reckoned she might not have minded if Melody had been much older than them. She looked about sixteen or seventeen, but Storm said she was fourteen, only a year and a bit older than herself, she thought angrily. At least Storm didn't much care for her. 'She thinks she's *so* special,' he sneered. Not that it really mattered what Storm thought. It was Effie who thought Melody was special, and that mattered. She was quite close to them now, and Cait hoped she would fall off one of the tussocks and get a wet foot.

'Daisy and Jason say they're going now,' she called out.

Storm was too far away, or too engrossed in eating, to hear. Bent over in the bushes, the boys looked like grazing sheep.

'I'll tell him,' Effie volunteered. Without warning, she stuck two fingers into her mouth and let out a piercing whistle. Cait covered her ears and Storm and his brothers jumped upright as if they had been stung.

'You're to go back,' shouted Melody. 'Daisy and Jason are going.'

Bounding over the brambles and bushes, Storm was with them in moments. 'Where? Where are they going?'

Melody shrugged. 'I dunno. They just said for me to come and get you.' With that, she turned on her pink plastic heel and walked daintily back towards the cattle grid. Effie waved, but Melody didn't turn round or notice her.

Picking the stickybacks off his shirt, Storm waited for his brothers. Cait looked at him in a 'what about us?' sort of way.

'You'd better come too,' he said.

Cait hesitated.

'Unless you'd prefer to stay here.'

The sight of Melody's pink behind wobbling its way up the sheep track was enough to make up Cait's mind. 'What will your parents say?'

Storm shrugged. 'Hey Effie, where did you learn to whistle like that?'

'Dad taught me.'

'Will you show me?'

'It'd be too difficult. Cait can't do it.'

Cait glared at Effie, trying to catch her eye, trying to give her a dirty look, but Effie kept staring straight ahead as they walked back.

Outside the bus, they could hear Jason and Daisy talking – quite loudly.

'We could be done for kidnapping,' Jason was saying.

'Hardly kidnapping.'

'That's not how the police might see it.'

'Then why don't you ask?'

'Ask who? Two little girls turn up in our bus and we don't rightly know from where.'

'They could be running away. Like Storm said,' Daisy argued.

'And you'd believe him! Like you always do. Half the time that boy lives on a cloud.'

'He doesn't mean any harm.'

'And neither do we. But that's not how it'd seem if we keep them. They're not ours.'

'Then you'll have to go to the police.'

'Me? Talk to the law? Are you joking? The way they work they'd have me in for 'questioning' as soon as look at me. They'd accuse me of this, that and the other, until sooner or later they'd find something that would stick. That's the way they work.'

It was the sort of thing Dad would say, Cait mused. He mightn't look like him, but sometimes Jason *sounded* like Dad. She hoped they could stay with them a bit longer.

'Well, have you a better idea?' Daisy said.

'I looked in the papers yesterday, when I was in the village. Nothing about two missing girls, but then there's not much of a selection down here. I'll look again tomorrow when we're nearer the cities.'

'So they can come then?' Daisy wheedled. 'Storm and the boys like them, and we've plenty of room.'

Jason sighed. 'It wouldn't be fair to ask one of the others to bring them in. And we can't just leave them. Not with some of the things you hear. You wouldn't know who might try to do them harm. I suppose they'd be safe with us at least. Till we find out whose they are.'

Outside the bus, Storm suddenly started panting. 'Make it look like I've been running,' he whispered to Cait. 'Don't want them to know we were listening.' He flung open the door. 'Melody says we're going.'

'Yeah,' said Jason, 'I've to meet my brother in Hereford.'

'Uncle Pete?'

'And Auntie Pat,' Daisy added.

'Woweee!'

'Are the boys with you?'

'They're coming,' Storm answered his mother. 'But they're awfully slow.'

With that, Deo and Rebus threw themselves into the

bus. Their panting was genuine.

'Water!' Deo whined, diving for the fridge.

'Where are the girls?' Daisy asked.

'Can they come too?'

Jason held up his hands. 'It's only temporary, now. Only temporary.'

'Woweee!' said Storm again. 'Come on in, Cait. We're off to see my Uncle Pete.'

Pushing Effie on ahead of her, Cait boarded the bus. She was relieved that they weren't being left behind, glad that they would soon be back on the road. She didn't feel excited though – not in the way Storm did – but there was a funny sort of chewing feeling somewhere in the pit of her stomach, like her life was about to be turned over, all over again.

As the jungly bus bumped and growled back up the rutted track, Cait felt a twinge of regret as the strange encampment disappeared behind a bend of the road. If she ever lived in a village, she decided, she hoped it would be like that; where you could just fit in as if a place had been laid for you. No questions, no history, you were just a part of their 'no trouble', 'no worries' present. In a way it was just as well that Jason and Daisy were moving on and taking herself and Effie with them; it would have been much harder to walk away from such relaxed carelessness on their own. But Effie was right; it was the end of their holiday; they should be back in Ireland by now. Dad had never actually said they'd be going to Clare as soon as they got back, but Cait was sure Nana and Granda would be expecting them.

They were on the smooth tarmac of the main road now, but the bus's engine seemed to strain as it crawled up the curve of a purple-cloaked moor. It was a bit like the Burren, near Nana's, Cait thought. The colours were the same: peaty browns, smoky mauves, the scorching yellow of gorse and the sheep that looked like rocks, Granda said, till they moved and surprised you.

Just as well Mam had phoned from the little library at the holiday place, the evening they got back from Spit Beach. Nana and Granda wouldn't mind if they didn't hear from them for a few days more. They'd probably think they'd be too tired after their journey home: that they'd be too busy unpacking. Mam often said, when they'd come back after the summer in Clare, that she'd be so exhausted with all the unpacking and washing, she'd wonder why people bothered to go on holiday at all. Holiday. Cait wondered whether they were still on one, her and Effie. Where were you, she thought, if you weren't at home and you weren't on holiday either? She looked at Effie and was glad to see her sister laughing. There was a song on the radio, 'Pretty Woman', and Deo and Rebus had put belts around their T-shirts and were mincing up and down the bus, pretending to be girls. Cait found herself smiling, then yawned.

'Tell Effie I'm going to lie down for a bit,' she said to Storm.

Behind the curtain, Cait flopped down on to the bunk she shared with Effie; stretching out on her back with her hands behind her head. It felt good to be on her own for a few minutes – it would give her time to think – if she could only hear herself think, over the noise of the radio and the boys keeping Effie laughing with their pop star imitations. Sitting up, she took out the map. If she could see where they were going, she might be able to plan where to go next. Finding Dartmoor was easy. It was the round purple bruise down on the toe of England. Devon's bunion, she said to herself, thinking about Nana when she'd complain about the bunions on her feet. She had to look harder to find Hereford, where Storm said his Uncle Pete was from. It was up near the zig-zaggy line that separated Wales from England. 'At least it's in the right direction,' she murmured to herself as she folded the map and stuck it back in the front pocket of her bag. It wouldn't go in easily; there was something in the way. Making space for the map, she took out a slim brown paper bag and remembered. The postcard she'd bought in the Sea-Life Centre back in Newquay; that seemed a million years ago now. Taking it out, she turned it over. It was a picture of two girls in the glass tunnel, with the sharks swimming over. She'd got it to send to Nana and Granda, because the girls, Effie said, were like her and Cait. Maybe she should still send it? They wouldn't worry if they heard from them. With Mam's pen from her bum-bag and resting on the back of her bag, Cait wrote: 'Having a great time. We're all well. Mam says 'Hi'. See you when we get back.' She had to pretend she was writing about someone else; like it was an exercise at school. It was only words. Not real lies. When Nana read this, she'd just think they were staying on holiday another week and wouldn't be worried. She put the card back in the bag with the map. When she got a stamp, she'd send it.

She yawned, and blinked, wanting to stay awake – to see where they were going – but she hadn't slept properly in days, and tiredness soon got the better of her. The last sign she noticed was the motorway exit for Bristol. When Storm eventually woke her, she was groggy and disorientated.

'We're at my Uncle Pete's,' he said.

Cait stretched, yawned and rubbed her eyes. Through

the window she could see the back of a house. The bus was stopped in what appeared to be a large yard at the back of a bungalow. Two huge dogs patrolled as far as their heavy chains would allow. A couple of chickens scratched unconcernedly in the shade of a rusty wheelbarrow. Stacked against the wall of the house was a pile of car doors. A brief look around the inside of the bus told her that it was empty. 'Where's Effie?' she said in alarm.

'Gone into the house with Rebus and Deo. Auntie Pat said she'd give them some of her apple juice. Do you want some? It's home-made. Not homogenised or nothing.'

'That's milk,' yawned Cait.

'Whatever,' said Storm happily. 'It's delicious.'

It *was* delicious, thought Cait, running her finger down the moisture on the side of the glass; sort of cloudy, with bits in it, but it tasted really appley. The smell reminded her of home, of the fruit that fell from the tree when the wasps had eaten holes in it. Storm's Auntie Pat was nice too; she said that if they wanted, they could use her bathroom to clean themselves up in. A nice way, thought Cait, of telling them they were all dirty! Jason and Storm's Uncle Pete, and another man they called Col, went back out to the yard and into the bus. Daisy told Rebus and Deo they weren't to follow them, that they were talking men's talk and it was none of their business. She kept them with her while she and Pat sat down, kicked off their sandals and stuck their feet up on a low table while they chatted. The TV was on, but no one was really watching it. Storm had a cousin, Giles, who looked old enough nearly to need to shave. He seemed sulky, like he wanted to be in the bus with the men, and when Storm kept talking and talking to him, he suddenly got up out of the squashy chair he'd been sprawled over, and left the room. He didn't say anything to them, but he knocked Mi Mi off the table as he was passing, for sport. Effie said nothing, but tried to give him one of her looks, as she climbed off her stool, retrieved the rabbit, brushed the dust and breadcrumbs off his fluffy pink fur and gave him a kiss. The floor was quite dirty. Cait reckoned Auntie Pat mustn't have been on such good terms with a sweeping brush as her mam was. She touched Effie's arm.

'Are you OK?'

Effie nodded. 'Are we staying here?'

'I don't know,' said Cait. 'Let's just see what happens.'

Storm's Auntie Pat made them chips and sausages that evening. Effie stared at her plate as if it was her birthday.

'You're not eating?' Cait nudged her.

Effie dug in. 'Magic stew is OK,' she said, through a mouthful of chips, 'but chips are better.'

The television was still on. The weatherman was announcing a drop in temperature, but still no sign of rain. Then it was the News, and, as if they'd been waiting for it, Jason, Uncle Pete and Col suddenly barged back in and stood in a ragged line, watching.

'It mightn't be on 'till the morning,' Uncle Pete said.

'And it might,' said Col. 'See, do they say anything about it?'

With them in the way, Cait couldn't see the television, but she heard that the reservoirs were at their lowest level and the farmers were looking for rain. There had been an accident at the Wellington turn off, and a bull had escaped from an abattoir and was going ballistic in a shopping centre. 'Looking for china shops,' Cait found herself dreamily thinking. Then there was a pause and the tone of the newsreader's voice dropped, like he was announcing something serious.

'This is it!' Col hissed to Uncle Pete.

'After making a gruesome discovery at a Cornish holiday premises last night,' the newsreader was saying, and Cait jumped as if she'd been pinched, 'police are considering the involvement of a Satanic cult ...'

'Nah ... It's not going to be on tonight.' Col appeared to be disappointed, but the men stayed watching anyway.

'Detectives are concerned by the presence of a large black cross at the scene and links are being sought to certain black magic rituals ...' The newsreader's voice had gone soft and kind of creepy.

Cait felt her heart begin to pound. 'Black magic!' her mind screamed. 'Now they think we're witches!' Surreptitiously she looked over at Effie, but her sister was quietly chatting to Mi Mi. The News never interested her. Cait strained, trying to listen, but the men were making too much noise. She only caught snatches: 'Police are seeking ...' and fragmented words like 'relatives' and 'information'. All too quickly, the television was turned off.

'You weren't down there in Cornwall?' Uncle Pete joked to Col.

'Black magic?' Col kind of sucked air between his teeth. 'Not my scene.'

'Well, that's it then,' said Uncle Pete. 'I said it wouldn't be on yet.'

Hoping her face showed none of the confusion she felt, Cait tried to make sense of the little she had heard. 'Relatives'. 'Information'. That meant they'd tell Nana and Granda. The postcard would be no good. Now they *would* worry. She must find a telephone and ring them, just as soon as she could.

They were shooed off to the bus early that evening.

"Night, kids.' Pete's friend Col smiled at Cait as he slammed the boot of his car. Cait flinched at the sound. 'Sorry about that,' he said. 'Catch is bust.'

Cait watched as he bent to pick up the box he'd removed from the car. From the weight of it and the unmistakable clinking sound, she knew what it contained. Col and the others were going to be drinking tonight.

'Are we going to stay here long?' Cait asked, as they sat around the table in the bus. 'With your Uncle Pete?'

'Don't think so,' Storm shrugged. 'Daisy says we're going to Ireland soon. I've cousins there.' He took down a stack of playing cards from a shelf.

'Ireland!' Effie suddenly piped up. 'That's where ...' Cait flashed her a stare, and she shut up.

'Can we come?' Cait tried not to appear excited.

'Dunno.' Storm started slowly shuffling the cards, with some difficulty since there seemed to be about four packs. 'I heard Jason saying something about sending you back.'

'Back! Back where?' Cait was alarmed.

'But don't worry,' Storm reassured her. 'He'll let you come. If I ask him right.' He began dealing the cards. 'Play Snap?'

Deo and Rebus nodded excitedly, and rather than feel left out, Cait joined in. He *will* let us, she told herself. He *must*. But as the rowdy game progressed, all such thoughts were soon banished.

'Isn't my Uncle Pete great?' Storm enthused, as they took a momentary breather. 'He owns this bus.'

'What does he do?' asked Cait, laying down the six of hearts.

'This and that,' laughed Storm. 'And sometimes a bit of the other, Jason says.'

'What's the other?' Effie asked. She wasn't playing cards; just sitting hunched in a corner, sucking her thumb and playing with Mi Mi's ears. Cait looked over at her and smiled, but Effie's head was down and she didn't see.

'Snap!' yelled Deo, thumping his two hands down on to the stack of cards.

Rebus grabbed him by the arm and pulled. 'You cheat!'

'Am not.'

'Are so. I saw you. You took that card from the bottom of your pile. You *knew* what it was.'

'Did not.'

'Did.'

'You're scabby.'

'You're scabbier.'

'Well, you're the scabbiest pea-brain that ever crawled out of a toilet!'

Rebus stuck his tongue out. 'Eunneugh!'

'You love Melody Smith.'

Suddenly the boys were on the floor, pulling, pushing and kicking. Cait circled the heap of cards with her arms to stop them being knocked to the floor. With his brothers still screaming at each other, Storm waded into the fray in a vain attempt to separate them. The three of them quickly formed a writhing mass as Storm tried keep them apart in the only way he could – by wedging his body between theirs – while avoiding their poking fingers, scratching nails and hard-kicking feet. Nobody heard the bus door opening or noticed Jason and Storm's Uncle Pete suddenly barge in.

'What the hell's going on?' Jason had a firm grip around Storm's upper arm, dragging him to his feet.

'Nothing,' Storm whined.

'You can be heard all over! Worse than hooligans. People in Birmingham don't want to be kept awake by you brats.'

'Sorry,' Storm tried to twist free. 'Ow! You're hurting.'

'And if I catch you fighting with your brothers again ...'

'I wasn't fighting!'

'Well, you weren't playing dominoes!'

'They were fighting. I was only ...'

'Only what!' roared Jason, shaking Storm hard. Cait wished she had the strength to butt in, tell Jason the truth, stand up for Storm just as he had for her. But she was afraid. It was the way Jason shouted at Storm that terrified her. He really *did* sound like Dad. She just couldn't move.

'Leave him,' Pete put a hand on Jason's shoulder. 'All boys fight.'

'I wasn't fighting,' Storm protested.

'Never you!' Jason shook him again. 'You make me sick!'

Pete tried to distract his brother; break the tension. 'Leave it, Jay. He's only a kid.'

'He's my kid,' Jason gave one last shove before letting go. 'And I'll do what I want.' Giving himself an indignant shake, Jason stormed out of the bus. Storm cowered in the corner by the curtain to his bunk. Effie and Mi Mi were curled together in a tight ball on the seat and Deo and Rebus were helping each other to drinks of water and trying to be as quiet as possible.

Pete turned to Cait. 'Can we have the cards, love. We want to play a game.'

Silently, Cait gathered the four packs of cards into one large bundle. Two-handedly she gave them to Pete. 'I think they're all there.'

The door slammed shut and suddenly Storm was up. He ran to the window, banging on the glass. 'I hate you!' he yelled. 'I wish you were dead!'

Cait's blood ran cold. Was that what she had wished?

chapter eight

The next day, the events of the previous evening seemed to have been forgotten. Cait woke late to the sound of Daisy tipping a bag of empty cans into the bin outside. Effie was sitting on the bed beside her. The boys were gone.

'You were tired,' Effie said. 'I let you sleep.'

Treating themselves to clean clothes from their bags, the girls dressed, wandered out into the yard and into the house.

'Morning, kids,' said Daisy. 'Do you want some breakfast?'

'Where's Auntie Pat?' Cait enquired.

Storm's Uncle Pete was sitting at the table, drinking a mug of coffee. 'She's gone to town. To work.'

Just then, Storm came bounding in. 'Jason says we can go to town. Do you want to come?'

Effie looked at Cait and Cait knew by the way her eyes suddenly sparkled, she wanted to go. 'OK then,' she said.

'Have some breakfast first,' suggested Daisy, pushing a

plate of toast towards them. 'Then you can go.'

In the small square at the centre of town, Cait, Effie and the boys piled out of the back of Uncle Pete's van.

'Now, you can hang around with us,' said Jason, 'or you can look around on your own.' He looked at his watch. 'But be back here in one hour.'

Storm and his brothers elected to go with their father. Cait decided she and Effie would explore together.

'Mind yourselves then,' said Storm's Uncle Pete. 'See you later.'

Cait patted the bum-bag under her jacket. The weather wasn't as warm as it had been yesterday. She did up Effie's buttons, not wanting her sister to catch cold.

'Where shall we go?'

'This way,' Cait replied, leading her sister around the corner and down a narrow street flanked with little shops that each looked like the gingerbread house in one of Effie's picture books. They walked until the shops gave way to plainer-looking houses, and Cait decided they should turn and go a different way.

'People round here must read a lot,' Effie remarked.

'Why do you say that?'

'There's an awful lot of bookshops.'

'I expect loads of smart people live here.'

'But what do they eat?' said Effie. 'You can't eat books.'

The smell of fresh baking drew them down in another direction. They stopped outside a bakery. Bread, buns and cakes of every description filled the window.

'My tummy says it's hungry,' Effie said. 'Can we get something?'

Cait bought them a sticky bun each with white icing and a cherry on top. They munched them straight out of the brown paper bag as they walked.

'Better even than chips,' Effie mumbled, her mouth a circlet of sticky white icing.

They stopped on the bridge that crossed the river. A family of ducks caught Effie's attention, and they went down for a closer look. Cait tipped the last remaining crumbs from the paper bag and, quacking loudly, the ducks waddled over to polish them off.

'They're like little hoovers!' Effie clapped her hands with delight.

'Maybe we should take one back to go under Auntie Pat's table,' Cait joked.

The crumbs were quickly gobbled up. 'Can we get some more,' Effie pleaded. 'They're starving.'

Cait nearly retorted that the ducks were just greedy, but Effie's smile was winning. 'Why not,' she said, delighted that her sister seemed so happy now.

On the way back to the bakery, they passed a newsagents. 'Can we get sweets?' Effie wheedled.

Cait smiled to herself, knowing well that Effie was intending to take full advantage of her present generous nature. 'Come on then.'

As Effie lingered over the banks of temptingly arranged packets, bars and tubes, Cait wandered over to the paper displays. Maybe she would treat herself to a magazine. Thumbing through the brightly coloured covers, a picture on one of the papers on the shelf below caught her eye and, with a stomach-churning jolt, she realised she was looking at herself and Effie. She glanced over her shoulder; her sister was still engrossed in choosing sweets. She took up a magazine, pretended to read it, while peering over it at the newspaper. 'MISSING' was the big black headline. Below the picture were their names, 'Caitlin and

Aoife Pengelly' and 'Have you seen these children?' She didn't have time to read on, because suddenly Effie was beside her, thrusting a packet of sweets towards her face.

'I've chosen,' she cried. 'Skittles. 'Cause they make me think of rainbows. What's that?' she pointed.

Cait fiddled under her shirt for coins in her bum-bag. 'Shut up,' she muttered. 'Pretend you haven't seen.'

'It's us, isn't it?'

'Shussh.'

'It *is* though. It is us.'

'Stop it,' Cait hissed. 'Just keep quiet. Act normal.'

Finding it hard to act normal herself, Cait handed up the money for the Skittles. She kept her head down, and as soon as the shopkeeper rang the till, she grabbed Effie's hand and made a bolt for the door.

'Hey!' the shopkeeper called after her.

Cait stopped, turned, hoping her hair would hide her face.

'Your change.' The shopkeeper leaned over the counter to deposit a few coins on to Cait's palm. 'Not like you kids to forget change.'

'No,' muttered Cait with a tiny half-smile. 'Thanks.'

'Byeee,' Effie had turned and waved, before Cait could stop her.

'What did you do that for?' she demanded, as soon as they were back on the street.

'He was a nice man,' Effie said simply. 'I liked his shop.'

'Come on,' Cait pulled her sister back down the narrow street, away from the newsagent, away from the newspaper with their faces on it. 'Before anyone else sees.'

Effie shared the Skittles, except the yellow ones, which she said were her favourite. 'If Nana and Granda saw that picture,' she munched thoughtfully, 'they'd be really worried.'

Cait nodded in agreement. She was thinking of the News on the television last night. 'We should ring them.'

'Didn't I say that already.'

'I know. And there should be a phone around here somewhere.'

'There's one down by the river. I saw it when we were feeding the ducks.'

'Come on then!'

The two girls ran, their shoes clattering on the pavement, back down to the river.

Squashed together in the glass cubicle, Cait hesitated, her finger poised over the dial. 'I don't know the number.'

''Course you do. You always know Nana and Granda's number.'

'That's when we're in Ireland,' Cait slowly replaced the receiver. 'It's different in England.'

'Does Nana and Granda's number change, then?' Effie looked worried, as if wondering what else might suddenly change.

'Not the last bit,' Cait reassured her. 'But you have to put different numbers in front. Depending where you are. Mam told me. She rang Nana's from the holiday place last week.'

'What different numbers?'

'I don't know. I can't remember. There were lots of them. Six or seven.'

'Dial six and seven then. See does that work.'

Cait smiled. Sometimes she wished she could be like Effie and not have to worry about everything. It mightn't be too bad looking after herself, but she had to look after Effie as well now. There was a phone book on the shelf under the phone. Cait pulled it out, screwing up her face in disgust as she flicked the dried-up bit of chewing gum off the front of it. Mam said you could look up most things in the phone book. Maybe the numbers to Ireland would be in it. She thumbed through the curled and yellowing pages, but someone had torn out all the pages that told you how to ring anywhere in the world.

'It's no good!' Cait threw the book back on the shelf.

'Couldn't we find another phone box?'

Cait looked out through the glass. The ducks had waddled up out of the river and were preening themselves on the bank. 'We could ask someone.'

There didn't seem to be anyone about. Only ducks.

'A pity they're not pigeons,' Effie had her nose to the glass. 'We could tie a note to a pigeon's leg.'

'Now you're being silly,' Cait giggled, aiming a playful swipe at her sister.

'Yeah,' admitted Effie. 'But I made you laugh.'

Just for a moment it felt good. The two of them here in a phone box, in their own little world. Sisters sharing a joke, just like they used to – before … Cait didn't even want to think about it any more. 'What do you think Baz and Ringo would do?'

Effie wrinkled her nose. 'Mexican bandits wouldn't use phone boxes, silly.'

'Well, what would they use? The Pony Express?'

'Nah. If Ringo wanted to call someone, he'd stride on down the street.' Effie stuck her thumbs into her jacket pockets and by swaying from side to side pretended she was swaggering down a street. 'Then he'd go right into the telegraph shop, and he'd say to the old woman behind the counter, "Lady, I wanna make a call," and then she'd take down the receiver,' Effie reached and took down the phone, 'pretend it's one of those old fashioned standy-up type things. Then she'd bang on the clicky thing.' Effie pressed the button a few times and using a squeaky old woman voice, yelled into the phone, 'Operator! Operator! Operator!'

'That's it!' said Cait. 'That's it. We'll ring the operator.' Grabbing the phone from her sister, she pushed back the half-torn label stuck on to the side of the phone box, so that she could read it. 'For operator assistance ...' She dialled the number and waited. 'Hello.' She forced cheeriness into her voice. 'I want to ring Ireland. Can you tell me the number to dial. I know the number – well the last bit anyway – but I need to know the numbers to put in front of it. No. I'll do it myself. Just give me the number. Hang on, I've a pen.' Thrusting the phone at Effie, she rummaged in her bum-bag for the pen she knew was there, and a piece of tissue. Her fingers felt all peculiar, like they were fat sausages, and she dropped the pen on the floor before she was ready. 'OK,' she took the phone back. 'I'm right now.' Carefully, to avoid tearing the tissue, she wrote the numbers, repeating each one back to make sure she had them all. 'Thank you,' she said at last. 'Thanks very much.' Replacing the receiver, she kissed the tissue before laying it out carefully on the shelf. 'Now we'll ring Nana.' Her hands were trembling as she fished into the bum-bag for the rest of their coins. There were only two fifty-pence pieces – they'd spent the rest on sweets and buns – but she hoped it would be enough. Taking a deep breath to calm herself, she lifted the receiver, pushed the coins into the slot, dialled the sequence of numbers and crossed her fingers. 'It's ringing,' she whispered to Effie. 'What'll I say?' Her heart was thumping, but her mind had blanked. It was easier writing words on a postcard than saying them out loud. How could she tell Nana not to worry and pretend that she and Effie were fine without starting to roar crying, with the telephone in her hand only accentuating the real distance between them? The phone stopped ringing. A tiny click as the receiver was lifted.

'Hello, Nana, it's me.' Cait's voice was suddenly very small.

'Is it Nana? Is it Nana?' Effie tugged at the hem of her jacket. Cait nodded. She was trying to listen.

'Yes, Effie's here too. With me. Say hello to Nana, Effie.' Cait held the receiver down.

'Hello, Nana.'

Taking it back quickly before Effie said too much, Cait cradled the receiver to her cheek, as if Nana was actually inside. 'We're both fine,' she said, blinking hard against the tears that were just starting to prick. 'So you don't need to worry.' She wiped her nose that was just beginning to run. 'We'll see you soon. Have the kettle on.' She smiled to herself. That was a phrase her mother always used.

'Let me talk again,' Effie insisted, grabbing the phone from her sister's grasp. Cait did not have the energy to fight back. Just now she was conducting her own private battle to keep her composure – for Effie's sake. Biting her lip, she focused blankly on the top of Effie's head. 'You have to speak,' she reminded. 'Nana can't hear you nodding.'

Effie looked up, the phone clutched in both hands. She looked worried. 'She wants to know where we are. Where are we?'

'The name of this place?'

Effie nodded, and panicked, Cait scanned the glass walls of the phone box, looking for clues. 'There's a sign by the ducks,' she said. 'Near the bridge.' She peered. It was a short word. Only three letters. 'W.Y.E.' 'Wye,' she said.

'Why?' Effie repeated into the receiver, her nose wrinkling.

She doesn't understand, thought Cait, grabbing the phone from her sister. 'Wye!' she said urgently. 'We're in Wye, Nana.'

There was no response Cait shook the receiver. 'It's dead!' she wailed.

'It went dead on me,' Effie said. 'I said "why" and it just died. I didn't do nothing.'

'I know,' Cait crouched, cradling her sister. 'It's OK Shushh. The money must have run out, that's all.'

Effie rubbed a fist across her eyes.

'At least Nana knows we're all right.' Opening the door, she took a welcome breath of fresh air. 'Come on. We'd better go back now. Or the others will have gone without us.'

Back at the square, they stared in disbelief. There were a dozen or so cars parked, but no white van. The others, it seemed, had indeed gone without them.

'Blast,' she said. 'And double blast.'

'What'll we do now?'

'Don't worry,' Cait reassured her sister. 'We'll walk. I know which road we came in on. I expect they'll come back for us. Then we can meet them on the way.'

There was no footpath, so Cait and Effie walked close to the verge, stepping back when cars passed to avoid being sprayed with loose gravel. A small stone got lodged in Cait's shoe and made her foot sore. Pulling Effie down beside her, she sat against the hedge while she tried to dislodge it. A grey car passed, then stopped and reversed back towards them.

'That's Col's car,' Effie observed.

'Oh good,' said Cait, relieved. 'Didn't I say we'd get a lift?'

Col wound down the passenger window, 'Hiya kids. Do you want a ride?'

Cait was on her feet in an instant. 'Yeah. Thanks.'

Effie grabbed her hand, squeezing her fingers. 'Cait,' she whispered. 'We don't know Col.'

'It's OK,' Cait assured her. 'Col's Pete's friend. Didn't we meet him last night?'

Effie still seemed reluctant.

'Don't be a wet. Pete probably sent Col out to fetch us. Didn't you, Col? Didn't Pete send you out?'

'Yeah. That's right.' Col had the passenger door open, and the front seat tipped forward. 'Are you getting in then, or what?'

Pushing Effie before her, Cait and her sister scrambled into the back of the car. 'Thanks,' she said. 'My feet were killing me.'

Col turned and smiled at the two girls before setting off again and Effie snuggled herself closer to her sister. It wasn't until they had gone some miles down the road that Cait had the uneasy feeling that they might have gone too far.

'Shouldn't we have turned off back there?'

Col turned and smiled again. Only this time it wasn't such a nice smile. It was a kind of leery smile that reminded Cait of the shark in one of the cartoons she and Effie liked watching. 'Thought we'd go for a drive.'

The car suddenly accelerated, the hedgerows whizzing past the windows in a greenish blur. Cait pressed her back to the seat, put her arm around Effie and prayed they wouldn't crash.

'Where are we going?' she ventured at last.

'You'll see,' said Col in a tight voice. 'Miss Caitlin and Aoife Pengelly.'

With a nauseous lurch, Cait realised that Col must have seen their picture in the paper.

chapter nine

The tiny wicket gate creaked as Col let them into the garden. Ahead of them, half-hidden by trees and bushes, was a tiny cottage. Privet hedges, once neatly trimmed, reared up on either side of the path, their leafy branches brushing against the girls as they passed. There didn't seem to be any other houses around, Cait noticed in dismay. This one was right at the end of an old lane, with grass growing up the middle and the scent of elder everywhere. Propelling them from behind, Col readied himself with the key, keeping them only a moment on the slate step before the door was open and they were pushed inside. Col flicked a switch and locked the door from the inside. The door was old and worn, and Cait thought it odd that the lock was so new and shiny. Pocketing the key, Col turned them around. They were in a small, rectangular hallway facing a yellowed door.

'The bathroom,' Col announced. The door grated, as if something was caught underneath, as Col pushed it open. 'In you go.'

Cait shook her head, tried to step back, and almost knocked into Effie.

'Come on,' Col insisted. 'You can go in by yourself. I won't look.'

'We don't want to go.'

''Course you do. Kids always want to go to the bathroom. Blowed if I'm going to start running up and down all night taking you. So you'd better go now.'

All night! Cait's mind echoed in horror, as she and Effie stepped into the bathroom with its lemon-yellow bath and black-and-white tiled walls. She closed the door with the tips of her fingers. 'It's very dirty,' she whispered.

Festoons of cobwebs hung from the ceiling and the bath was full of dust and black spots. Cait tore a bit of newspaper from a pile on the floor and wiped the toilet seat. 'You go first.'

Effie peered doubtfully into the brownish water, but settled herself nonetheless. Just then a loud scratchy noise made them both jump.

'What is it!'

Cait looked and listened as the scraping noise came again. She laughed. 'It's OK. Only the trees brushing against the window. Look.'

It would be almost impossible for the frosted window to let in any light, the hedge seemed to have grown up so close to it. A few strands of ivy had found their way through the small top opening and hung down over the cistern.

'It's like being in a jungle,' Effie whispered.

'Are you finished in there?' Col banged on the door.

'Nearly.'

The girls washed their hands under the dribble of cold water that was all they could get from the tap and timidly opened the door. There was a room on either side of the hall. Peeping into one and seeing a small table and a greasy-looking cooker, Cait knew it was the kitchen, but Col pushed them into the other room. Cleaned up, Cait thought, it could be the front room. Mam always kept the front room tidy for visitors – not that they ever had visitors, apart from the priest, when Dad was out – but this room was dirty and had hardly any furniture. There was only a knobbly-looking sofa with bits sticking out, a wooden chair with arms and a tatty rug in front of a fireplace filled with cigarette ends and polystyrene containers.

'Welcome to my 'umble abode,' Col said in a funny accent that might have made Cait laugh if she didn't feel quite so scared. 'Do sit down.'

'Do you live here?' Cait's tone was incredulous, as she tried to make herself comfortable on the lumpy sofa.

Col laughed. 'Let's just say it's one of my homes.'

'Why, how many do you have?' Apart from bringing them here, Col hadn't actually been nasty to them and Cait hoped that if she acted nice, then so would he.

Col tapped the side of his nose. 'That'd be telling.'

'Is he rich?' Effie whispered, nudging in closer to her sister.

Col heard and laughed. 'Nah. I'm not rich. More's the pity. But I'm hoping your folks are.'

Cait stiffened. She wished she'd had a chance to read the article in the paper herself. 'Our folks are dead.'

'I know, I know.' Col's voice was vaguely sympathetic as if commiserating with them on the death of a hamster or something. 'Tragic, that's what it is. Tragic.'

'What is?' Effie hissed at Cait.

'You are, my love. You are. Out alone and far from home. But wait – 'Col paused dramatically, pulling a folded newspaper from his jacket pocket – 'not entirely alone.' He pointed to them and the single word 'MISSING'. 'Someone wants you back. Bad enough to put this in the papers. Reckon them that wants something bad enough will pay for it.'

'There's no one in our family who's got any money. And since you can't get nothing from nothing, you won't make a penny out of us.' Cait folded her arms resolutely, fixing him with her best 'so there' sort of look.

Col did not seem convinced. He just wagged his finger at her and tut-tutted, before trying to attract Effie's attention. Effie was tucked up beside her sister, twisting a knot of hair over her ear.

'Well, little girl.'

'Her name is Effie,' Cait said archly.

Col looked up sharply. 'I wasn't talking to you.' He bent his head down to Effie's level. 'Well, Effie. Is your granny rich?'

'She's not talking to you either,' Cait snapped.

'One more word from you,' Col snarled. 'And I'll …' he shook his fist at her, but Cait held her ground.

'I'm not afraid of you.' She tried to sound brave, but hoped her voice wouldn't give her away. It was as if a lump had settled in her throat, like she'd eaten something that wouldn't go down. The lump was trying to climb back up, right to the back of her mouth. She mustn't let it. She must keep the lump down. Col must not know she was afraid. Effie must not know. He was talking to her again in a wheedly softy voice.

'Has your granny got a big house?'

Effie kept her mouth tightly shut.

'I bet she gives you nice pressies.'

Effie screwed her eyes closed.

'Never mind.' Col sat back on the other chair and with long, bony fingers, extracted a pack of cigarettes and a box of matches from the pocket of his checked shirt. He took one, gripped it between his thin lips, and with the faint hiss as the match ignited, Cait thought suddenly of Dad. She loved that sound. It meant closeness. She could even smell his tobacco – as if the tin were open in front of her – a sort of sweet, composty smell. She could see him now, the bit of paper balanced in his fingers, teasing out a narrow sausage from the matted black lump. Then quick as a light, he'd roll it into a tight white tube, lick it closed and give it to Cait. She'd look to see how good it was. Most times it was eight or nine, but sometimes a perfect ten. Dad let her try and roll them sometimes, but hers were never very good; no more than a three at most. But by far the best bit was when she'd put it between his lips; he'd give her the match and she would light it. You had to get close for that, or the flame would go out. Dad would cup his hands around hers and draw them up, and just as the match lit the cigarette, they'd be so close, their heads sometimes touched. But then there'd be the first curl of eye-watering smoke and Cait would cough and pull away. She could smell Col's cigarette now, but it wasn't like the smoke Dad's used to make. It was the smell of old men in a pub and she didn't like it.

Col leaned back blowing a smoke ring at the ceiling. 'Then of course there'd be the redundancy.' He looked at Cait, who flinched, caught off guard. 'What was he going to do with that money? Your Dad.' Cait's expression was of blank confusion. 'You didn't know? I read it in the paper. Your Daddy got a lot of money. Let go only last month. Seems like the mining company gave him a right good package. He can hardly have spent it all yet. Reckon you two must be worth some of that.'

Her bum-bag suddenly felt huge beneath her shirt, but Cait steeled herself. 'Our Dad's dead.'

One eye half-closed from the smoke from his cigarette, Col raised an eyebrow – a narrow, pointed arch.

'Then he won't be needing it, will he?' Col stubbed his cigarette out on the arm of his chair and flicked the butt into the black hole of the fireplace. He seemed jumpy, thought Cait. Or maybe he was always like that. He stood up, stretched and hitched his jeans up over his bony hips. 'In the meantime you two can stay with me. Be my guests, if you like. See what sort of reward is put up. Don't worry. There's no one will find you here. Not unless I tell them. And I'm not going to tell them till I see the colour of their money.'

'Jason, or Storm's Uncle Pete will wonder where we are.'

'No, they won't.'

'What do you mean?'

'I mean,' Col explained, 'I told them I saw the police pick you up back there in town. Stands to reason, don't it? You being missing persons and all that. Tell you one thing. Jason was relieved. Saved him from having to bring you in himself. 'Cause sooner or later, Daisy would have made him. He'd hate that. All them questions. And he not being over-fond of the police at the best of times.'

'We don't like them neither. They put you in homes.' Effie spoke in a very small voice.

'It speaks!' Col exclaimed, as if Effie's talking was a miracle. Effie reddened and tucked her head back under her sister's arm. Col leaned over and tickled the back of Effie's neck. 'Don't know about you, but I'm starving. You'd eat chips, wouldn't you?'

Cait stared at him, stony-faced.

'I'd say yes if I were you,' Col suggested. 'It could be a long night.'

'OK,' Cait said, her mouth barely moving.

'OK,' Col echoed. 'Is that the best you can do?' Arms folded, Col stood in front of them. 'If you want me to buy you some chips, least you can do is ask nicely.'

'Asking nicely, OK.'

'Oh no, no, no, no,' Col shook his head. 'That won't do. Won't do at all.' Cait could see Col was enjoying himself, teasing her. Don't rise, she told herself. 'Don't let him see he's getting to you,' echoed her mother's voice in her head, like when she was being told to stand up to the bullies at school. 'Now,' Col continued. 'You have to say, 'Please Uncle Colin, we'd love some chips'.'

Cait grimaced. 'Uncle Colin. Please can we have some chips?'

'Say please.'

'I did.'

'Say it again.'

'Pleeese.'

'Pretty please.'

'With sugar on top.'

'That's better. See, you can be nice when you want to.' Col rattled the car keys in his pocket. 'Right then. Chippie's just down the road. I'll only be gone a few minutes. And in case you're thinking of escaping. Don't bother. The door will be locked and there's bars on all the windows.' He grinned. 'Can't trust anyone around here.'

The door slammed, and for a moment Cait felt like running to the window and yelling out after him, just like Storm had the previous evening. But her body felt heavy and unresponsive. She started to shiver and couldn't stop. She grabbed her legs up to her chest and sank her head down on to her knees. Like a hedgehog after danger has passed, Effie slowly uncurled. Cait felt her hand, wet and sticky, tapping at her cheek.

'Don't cry, Cait. Don't cry.'

'I'm not crying,' Cait looked up as if to prove it. The lump was still in her throat and the pricking sensation in the corners of her eyes reminded her that tears were not far away. But she wasn't crying. She wouldn't cry. She must be strong. She banged her head up and down on her knees.

'Cait, don't.'

'I'm just knocking my brain back into place.'

'You'll hurt yourself.'

'Who cares. I've been so stupid.' Cait clenched and unclenched her hands in the way Granda told her she should any time she felt angry. 'Look at the mess I've got us into. It's all my fault. You didn't want to go with Col. It was my idea. Now I've ruined everything.'

Effie was lightly stroking the downy hair on Cait's fore-arm. 'I don't think you're stupid, Cait. I think you're very clever.'

'So clever I've got us both locked up in a horrid little house with a man we don't like.'

Effie didn't say anything but carried on rubbing Cait's arm.

'What are we going to do now?' Cait wailed.

'What would Baz do?'

Cait looked at her sister, her face a mixture of exhaustion and despair. 'Baz has gone,' she said. 'He can't help any more. This is just down to us.'

Effie slipped from the sofa. 'Come on, then. Let's look around.'

Reluctantly, Cait unfolded her legs and stood up. 'It's no use, Col said everything was locked or barred.'

'Maybe he's missed something,' Effie encouraged. 'Come on.'

There was another door leading off the sitting room where they were. Cautiously Cait pushed against it, and blinked at the darkness of the room beyond. Its smell was a curious mixture of damp and human sweat. She flicked the light switch. It was a small room and dark because its two windows were completely boarded up. There was nothing in it except a large unmade bed and piles of clothes. Switching out the light the girls scuttled backwards and shut the door.

'It stinks!' exclaimed Effie, holding her nose.

There was nothing new to explore in the sitting room, so they crossed the hall to the kitchen. The window above the sink was crossed with bars and the wooden back door fastened with a padlock.

'That's it,' said Cait, rattling the lock in frustration. 'We're stuck here.'

'What about the bathroom?'

'We've seen that already.'

Nevertheless, since they were passing, they looked in again. The top flap window was still open.

'Bet I could get through that.'

'Don't be silly, Effie. It's tiny!'

'So am I.'

'You're not that thin.'

'Am so.' Effie pulled up her T-shirt, displaying a bare midriff. She wiggled her belly button and sucked in her stomach. 'Look how thin I am, Cait. I could squeeze through that window.'

Cait looked, measuring with her eyes the width of her

sister and the narrowness of the window. 'But what about me?' she said. 'I couldn't get through the window. I'd still be stuck.'

Effie dropped her T- shirt. 'Well, that's no good then.'

A sudden noise sent them scarpering back to the sofa. They heard the whine of the gate and knew Col must be back. He greeted them both with a brown paper bag of chips. The smell of hot grease and vinegar permeated the room. Suddenly, in spite of Col being a stranger and all that, they were ravenous.

'You OK, kids?'

The girls nodded, their lips pursed around steaming potato.

'Not scared or nothing? Being left on your own.'

'We're not scared of anything,' Cait said bravely.

'Nor me neither,' said Col. 'Except ghosts.'

Cait shivered involuntarily.

'Have you ever walked past a graveyard late at night,' said Col. 'Brings me out in a cold sweat, it does. Daytime, no problem. But night-time – whuuurr! That's when the ghosts come out, see. After dark. Don't like moths, neither.'

Effie giggled. 'Moths are only night-time butterflies.'

'That's as maybe,' Col said. 'But did you ever have one this size,' he held his fingers about six inches apart, 'get caught up under your hair and it flap-flapping trying to get out?'

Effie shook her head.

'Well shut up then, you don't know what you're talking about.'

They munched in silence, and when he'd finished, Col screwed up his bag and lobbed it into the fireplace. Effie wanted to throw hers as well, but Cait said no. She rubbed the bags over their fingers to clean them, then placed them gently on the hearth. Col sniffed to show he disapproved, then sat back with his hands behind his head, watching them. Cait felt uncomfortable. She didn't like the way he was looking at her. She tried to look anywhere else: at Effie, sitting expressionless and silent, at the thin, flowery curtains that were growing steadily darker as day gave way to evening. All the time she could feel Col's eyes boring into her. She bit her fingernail. Don't let him get to you, she told herself, over and over.

Suddenly Col yawned, a loud scratching yawn and she jumped.

'I left a message with my mate Jed. He said he'd ring the police. See about a reward for you two. Reckon it'll be morning before we hear anything though. Time for a bit of shut-eye.'

'I'm not tired,' Cait lied.

'It'll be a long night without sleep.' As Col passed the sofa, he brushed her shoulder with his hand, tickled the skin above the scoop neck of her shirt. Cait shuddered, then found herself shaking all over. Col ran his fingers down her arm. It felt like they were burning tracks in her skin. She wanted to scream, but she couldn't even open her mouth. She wanted to shout, No! No! No!, but, except for a tiny mewling squeak coming from the back of her throat, she was mute. She couldn't even turn her head to see her sister. She just sat there, frozen, while Col's creeping fingers raised goose-flesh all the way up and down her neck.

Suddenly a noise beside her broke the spell. Effie had rolled off the sofa, groaning, clutching her stomach with one hand, her mouth with the other. Col jumped back in alarm. 'Jesus Christ! She's not going to die on me!'

Cait was down beside her sister, even before she knew how she'd got off the sofa. Frantically she tried to feel her forehead, feel for a pulse, do something. Effie groaned, her eyes rolling so that the whites showed.

'Effie! Effie! Are you OK?'

From between a crack in the fingers clamped over her mouth, Effie squeaked two words, 'cat's sick,' and Cait understood. Ever since Blackie got sick behind the cooker and Mam nearly got sick trying to clean it up, they used that word when they feigned illness, and it drove her mad.

'She's going to be sick,' she said in a fake panic. 'It's the chips! If Effie eats chips not cooked in corn oil, she gets sick!'

'God Almighty! Don't let her puke in here!' In two strides, Col had crossed the floor, picked up Effie by the shoulders and frog-marched her to the bathroom. From behind the closed door, they could hear Effie gagging and choking.

'She'll be OK, once it's out,' Cait reassured Col, whose face had gone quite green.

The sound of Effie disgorging was too much for him. 'Bloody kids,' he said in disgust. 'Turn your stomach. Let me know when she's finished.' Col retreated back into the sitting room, leaving Cait wavering in the hall. There were some minutes of silence, then came a sudden loud banging on the front door that made them both jump.

'That'll be Jed,' Col said, bounding up. 'He'll have news for me about the money.'

Hurriedly taking the key from his pocket, Col turned the lock and as the door opened, Cait, hovering just behind Col, could see nothing but the back of his blue-and-red checked shirt. It stank of tobacco and the smell of his bedroom. The sudden blast of cold, but fresh, air crashed into her like a wave.

'Jed?' Col called out into the dark. 'Are you there, man?'

The wicket gate creaked on its hinges. There was a slight scuffling noise from the overgrown hedge. Col bent and picked up two stones. 'Bloody rats,' he cursed, lobbing a stone into the hedge. 'Who's out there?'

'Must have been a ghost.' Cait was feeling quite scared herself.

Col tightened his jacket. 'Don't you bloody start.'

Just then a cat called. A long, drawn out 'miaooow'. Col lobbed the other stone. 'Bloody cats an' all.'

Suddenly Cait knew. From all the games of 'hunt in the dark' they'd played, she knew that call. As Col bent down for another missile, Cait seized her chance. She slipped out by him, dodged his hands reaching up to grab her, ran down the path, through the gate and almost crashed into Effie who was crouched behind the hedge. Without a word to each other, the two girls sprinted down the lane, Cait pulling Effie by the hand to keep her going faster. Passing a field gate, they slithered and rolled through the bars and lay flat amongst tall corn stalks. With their mouths shut to stop their breath escaping loudly, the girls heard the ominous thud-thudding of Col's heavy-footed pursuit. The footsteps passed the gate and Cait squeezed Effie's hand to remind her to keep quiet. When she couldn't hear the footsteps any more, she felt like shouting for joy. She knew he'd be back, though, and they weren't safe yet. 'Come on,' she whispered to Effie. 'We can't stay here.'

Like frightened mice, the two girls scampered and crept along by the hedge. They crossed the field and two more besides, coming to a panting stop at the foot of a high stone wall. However, using overhanging branches and the strength of their fingertips, they managed to scale the wall and drop down into long grass the far side. Ahead of them, looming large in the yellow light from a street somewhere, a row of unmistakable shapes.

'It's a graveyard!'

Effie clung to her sister in alarm.

'We could stay here. He'd never find us here. He's scared of ghosts.'

'Cait,' squeaked Effie. 'I'm scared of ghosts too.'

chapter ten

By the light of a sickly moon, Cait looked around. They were right at the edge of the graveyard, sheltered by the wall and a row of huge trees. There were plenty of dry twigs.

'We'll make a little fire.'

'Won't someone see the smoke?'

'Only a little one,' Cait reassured her. 'The smoke will be hidden by the trees.'

Quickly they scraped together a small pile, and using Dad's lighter and an old tissue from her bum-bag, Cait managed to coax a small flame into life.

'That's better,' Effie said happily. 'Now nothing will come near us.'

'I was scared back there,' Cait admitted. 'Really scared.' Effie twisted her head round and smiled. 'But you, you rescued me. You brave little thing, you.'

Effie grinned and sighed with a drama Storm would have envied. 'It was nothing.'

'You weren't really sick?'

'Nah. I was just pretending.'

'And you got out through the window?'

'I wriggled and I squiggled. And I nearly squeezed out of my knick-knacks. And look …' Effie lifted her T-shirt. In the light of the fire flame, Cait could plainly see the line of livid red bruising all down her sister's front.

'What happened?'

'I forgot about the knob for the window catch. It nearly gutted me!'

'Is it sore?'

'Just a bit. But …' Effie beamed at her sister. 'I don't mind, really.'

For a while the girls sat in silence, listening to the creak, creak of the branches above them and the gentle spit and crackle of their little fire. Effie shivered, and realising she must have had to leave her jacket to get out through the window, Cait took hers off and wrapped it around her sister.

'That better?'

'Mmmm,' Effie murmured.

'Lucky we had clean clothes this morning,' Cait observed. 'We left our bags on the jungly bus.'

'We left Mi Mi as well.'

'Will you be all right?'

'Think so. Mi Mi wouldn't like it here anyways. He'd be scared.'

'But you're not scared?'

Effie didn't answer for a moment, then came a small voice, 'Well. I am. Just a bit,' she admitted.

'That's OK.' Cait stroked her hair. 'I'll mind you.'

Effie slipped into a thoughtful silence. She was lying across Cait's legs, snuggled under Cait's jacket and staring blankly at the nearest line of headstones. The air was still, and apart from the hiss and fizz of leaves on their little fire, there was no sound. Like Effie, Cait stared out at the tangled ivy that had wrapped itself around the base of the nearest headstone, telling herself that graveyards were not really scary places. Just somewhere where people could sleep for ever, without being disturbed. She wished she could sleep now. Sleep and wake to comfort, as from a bad dream. But she *hadn't* been dreaming. Things really *had* happened. Terrible things. Like lightning flashes, the images came: a rubbish-filled fireplace; a greasy cooker; black-and-white tiles around a dirty yellow bath; a red-and-blue checked shirt; Col and his horrible breath, leaning over her. Then behind him, the faded wallpaper turned ice green and she could see red like spattered ketchup, pink of a bedspread, half on the floor, then the black of Dad's big overshirt, as in her head she heard shouts, screaming and through it all, an ear-shattering crack like a dry stick breaking. She could feel her body shivering and tried desperately to lead her mind elsewhere.

More jumbled images flooded her mind. The foam-edged tongues of sea that licked the beach at Newquay became the grey-blue tongues of cattle licking away dripping saliva as the beasts drank from the water-trough in the field behind the holiday place. Clouds of flies shaken from their heavy heads became glass-bodied shrimps, rocked by the tide. And the diamond-bright, sugary sand that stuck to the skin of her legs, became a starry constellation. Mam and Dad were up there in the stars, she thought wistfully, along with all the souls that had gone before. Along with those of all the people left to sleep in this graveyard. And in their midst, she and Effie – two living souls – rocked like the shrimps, caught in the drift of the dead.

Her thoughts finally brought her to the day last week when, after dropping Mam off in town to do some shopping, Dad said he would take them to visit their other grandparents. Effie had been terribly excited, so had Cait – even though she thought it a bit odd – as Dad had never really talked about his parents before.

'Do you think Grandad Pengelly will be tall, like Granda?' Cait remembered Effie asking.

Dad didn't say. He said they would go visiting first. He took them to a house where he said his parents once lived. Where he and his brother – their Uncle Robert – were brought up. It was in the middle of a grey terrace of barefaced cottages that clutched the earth between a narrow road and the steep-sided hill behind them. Number seven. Dad said they didn't live there anymore – he didn't know who lived there now – so they called to the people at number eight. They were an old couple, smaller and stouter than Nana and Granda, but Dad seemed pleased to see them. They were the Truscotts, Dad said, but he called them Kitty and Horace. Perched on high stools in the slate-floored kitchen, they all drank tea and ate scones, while Kitty Truscott kept staring at Effie and Cait. 'She's got your mother's ears,' she'd said to Dad. 'But the maid,' (meaning Effie) 'she don't look like your side at all.'

Horace beckoned Dad upstairs then, and when they came down, Dad was carrying a small case. Effie fixed on it straight away.

'What's that, Dad?'

Dad put the case on the table, running his fingers down the length of the dark leather.

'It's got Cait's name on it, Dad. C.P.' Effie touched the engraved letters. 'Cait Pengelly. Is it Cait's, Dad?'

Dad shook his head and Kitty Truscott laughed. 'No,

child,' she said. 'That C is for Charlie. Your dad's dad. It were his box.'

'What's in it?'

Dad loosened the buckles, opened the lid. The girls peered inside. Even in its two pieces, the shape was unmistakeable. 'A gun!' Effie had gasped. 'Was Grandad Pengelly a bandit?'

'He was not,' Horace interrupted, shutting the box, before Effie's excited fingers got a chance to explore. 'He was in the war. His medals and bits and pieces are in there as well,' he told Dad. 'Charlie asked me to keep them for you. Before he –'

'Before he what?' Cait had asked, suddenly.

'Before he went into the hospice.'

Cait had frowned.

'It's a place where you can be looked after,' Kitty explained, 'when you can't look after yourself no more.'

'Like a Home?' Cait had said.

'Are we going to see Gran and Grandad Pengelly now?' Effie wheeled, when finally they climbed back into the car.

'Wait and see,' was all Dad would say.

In the car, Effie asked lots of questions, none of which Dad answered properly. Effie didn't seem to mind, though; she just carried on asking. Cait, however, felt strangely uneasy, and when Dad pulled up beside a tiny church surrounded by towering yew trees, she knew she should have expected something like this. After leading them through the long and tussocky grass of the graveyard, Dad brought them to stand in front of a plain granite headstone.

'Say hello to your Gran and Grandad Pengelly.'

Effie's disappointment was loud. 'Dad, you tricked us. That's not fair.'

'Dead or alive, they're still your grandparents.' Dad then took a photo from his wallet. It was taken on the same day as the one Cait now had in her bum-bag, but it was one Mam took, so it was just of Dad with her and Effie. He put it down in front of the headstone and placed a bit of a slate on top, so it wouldn't blow away.

'That's so they'll always remember you,' Dad said.

Cait had shivered and couldn't wait to get out of the graveyard. On the way back, both she and Effie were feeling grouchy, so they annoyed each other on purpose. Effie said Cait was taking up too much space and Cait said Effie was only a little squirt and what did she need more space for anyway? Dad shouted at the two of them, and Cait complained that it was Effie's fault, because she'd started it, and Effie sat and sulked the whole way back to the holiday place. Later that night, Cait remembered lying awake listening to loud voices and slamming doors and reckoned that Mam was being cross with Dad for bringing them in the first place. It was a pity all the same, Cait mused as she threw a few more small sticks on the fire, that Dad's parents weren't alive. She would like to have met Gran and Grandad Charlie Pengelly.

'Cait?'

Cait came back from being a mile away. 'What?'

Effie shifted her position. She sniffed and rubbed her nose.

'Was Dad going to shoot us?'

Stunned into silence, Cait couldn't answer.

'He was, wasn't he? He had the gun pointed.'

Cait began to shake. The memory of that moment, that terrible, terrible moment, once again crashed its raw image across her brain: Mam's bare feet, Dad's face, twisted, red and sweating. And the gun. Grandad Pengelly's gun. The gun that was in two pieces. The gun that Horace Truscott didn't want them to see. Was that the gun Dad had? What was he thinking when they went to the Truscotts? What was he thinking – *then*? The awful dizziness of that moment was taking over again.

'Why?' Effie said.

Cait felt her mind would trip itself over, there was so much going on in her head. She could hear voices amongst the screams and shouts. Snatches of an argument. 'You can't take them away!' It was her dad's voice. 'They're my kids too!' It was the night after they came back from Newquay, and Dad was shouting, 'There's nobody takes my kids. Not you. Not nobody!'

'I think he was afraid of losing us.'

Effie thought for a moment. 'But he didn't, did he? Shoot us, I mean.'

Through the tears she couldn't hold back, Cait could see Dad now. Sweat slicked his face, but he wore his anger like a mask. She saw now the fearful look, the pain in his eyes. 'He didn't want to hurt us,' she said, as if speaking in a dream. 'He loved us. Really, he loved us.'

'I love him too,' mumbled Effie sleepily. 'And Mam and Nana and Granda. And you.'

Cait leaned down and planted a light kiss on the scruffy blonde head. 'But don't tell Granda about what he did,' she whispered. 'Nor Nana neither.'

Effie's eyes were closed. Cait leaned back against the rough bark of the yew tree. Why had she said that? Told Effie not to tell? What was it with Dad and Nana and Granda? Dad never stayed long when he left them out at Nana and Granda's. He said it was because of work. But *Mam* stayed. Then there was the way Granda never spoke to him till he was going. Funny, she'd never really noticed that before. Was it because Nana and Granda didn't *like* Dad? They liked Uncle Robert, though. Once, when Effie was a baby and Dad was bringing them for the summer, Uncle Robert came too. He made Nana laugh. Cait remembered how the flowers on her apron went up and down as she giggled until she had to use the corner of it to wipe her eyes. And when Dad and Uncle Robert were going, Granda shook his hand, clapped his back and said, 'Anytime!', like he really meant it. Maybe Dad didn't like that. *She* didn't like it when Effie went off with Melody Smith down on Dartmoor to paint their faces. Why couldn't things be easy like they used to be? Why couldn't she just stop worrying and go to sleep – like a baby? She felt exhausted. As if she'd been swimming with weights on her feet and had to struggle to reach the side. She wanted to cry – but no, not yet. Effie needed her, and not like that. Her breath was coming now in huge spasmodic lurches, as if her chest wanted to explode. God, what she wouldn't give to be in their own special bed in Nana's attic room, looking out through the gable window at the little rocky beach where she and Effie would play all summer, listening to the raucous call of gulls and the way they'd thump across the roof like they weighed ten ton. And then the smell. Cait sighed deeply, remembering. Outside it was a mixture of bogwater and salt, but inside it was the smell of rashers cooking and Nana's home-made bread, steaming hot from the oven. She hoped it wouldn't be too much longer before they got there. Right now she didn't even know where they were. The map was in her other bag, and she'd left that on Storm's bus.

Cait didn't remember falling asleep, but she woke early with the cold. Pale fingers of morning were spreading out along the horizon; the fire was nothing but a small heap of powdery grey ash and her neck was stiff.

'Come on, Effie,' Cait roused her sister. 'It's time we were going.'

'What time is it?' Effie yawned, without even opening her eyes.

'I don't know. But it'll be morning soon, and Col's only afraid of graveyards in the dark.'

The two girls stood up and brushed off the worst of the dry dust and leaves. Effie kicked at the remains of their fire, sending up a fine cloud of grey dust all over her shoes and legs.

'Effie, don't! You'll get yourself all dirty again.'

Effie stood while Cait batted at the pale film of dust, but to no avail: it stubbornly refused to leave her skin. 'It's no good,' she said. 'You look like a ghost.'

'Col won't come near me, so,' Effie said happily.

They walked up to the higher ground at the centre of the graveyard and looked around. Roughly square-shaped, the road on two sides met with another at the corner, where there was a chip shop, a tiny post office, three petrol pumps and a couple of modern bungalows. It was early – shutters, blinds and curtains were closed – there was no one about.

'I think we should stay off the road, all the same,' Cait decided. 'In case Col comes looking for us.'

'Do you think we should pray?'

Where the graveyard gave way to a meadow, a squat, rough-stone church hugged the corner.

'Mam would want us to pray,' Effie insisted.

That was true, Cait thought. Mam was always telling them to pray. To pray that Nana and Granda would keep well, that Dad would keep his job, that they'd be kept safe.

Glistening with dew, it was as if a slab of ice roofed the church. Like black eyes, its windows seemed to watch them. Cait hesitated.

'Or is it Dad's God that lives there?' Effie added.

Cait shrugged. 'I don't know.' She began to pick her way down from the hill. 'Anyway, I don't feel much like praying.' She turned. Effie was following her down. 'But you can if you like.'

The church looked bigger when they were beside it. Effie craned her neck looking up at the stone carved faces, that, open-mouthed, stared down. 'I don't feel like praying, either,' she said. 'I just said what Mam would say. That's all.'

'I know,' Cait sympathised, catching her sister's hand. 'Let's go this way.'

There was a stile behind the church, leading into the field. 'It must be a footpath,' said Cait, noticing the faint line of trampled earth. 'For people taking a short cut.'

They crossed the field, squeezed through a broken-down gate tied up with string, into the next field, over two more stiles, and came up right behind two huge polytunnels that hugged the ground like enormous fat maggots. Hearing voices, the two girls instinctively crouched down, quiet and still. They didn't want to get caught again. When the voices didn't come any nearer, and realising that it was nobody out looking for them, they picked a stealthy course down the side of one of the polytunnels, with Cait hoping that their shadows wouldn't be reflected inside. At the other end of the tunnel was a large steel water tank which hid them while they were able to look around. They were on a farm. The polytunnels were in a small field beside the yard. The farmhouse was down a few steps. All the curtains seemed to be closed, but two cats were drinking from a bowl at the farmhouse door. A third cat had its leg twisted up, as if it was playing a cello, Mam always said, while it licked itself. Between the yard and the poly-tunnels was a green van, with its back doors open. Then there was that smell. Even from where she was hiding, Cait caught the scent. Sweet but not sickly. She couldn't identify it at first, but it reminded her of one of the bubble-baths Mam used to get for them. It wasn't bubble-bath though. Her stomach was beginning to rumble, like it was telling her it was something edible, and she hoped it wouldn't do one of its gurgly tummy rolls and make Effie giggle. She listened hard. There were only two voices and they seemed to be coming from the tunnel next to them.

'You'd want to get a move on, Martin. Market'll be open in an hour.'

'I've just got this one more tray. Then I'm gone.'

Two men came out of the tunnel, carrying a wooden board between them and Cait knew instantly what she had been smelling. Strawberries! Rows of blue punnets, packed with the biggest, ripest, most delicious-looking strawberries she'd ever seen. Her mouth was already watering in anticipation. The men put the tray into the back of the van.

'That's it then. Are you ready now?'

'My jacket's in the kitchen. I'll just get that and go.'

Cait watched the two men cross the yard and go down the few steps to the house. There didn't seem to be anyone else around. Apart from the cheeping of quarrelsome sparrows in the trees around the yard, there was no other sound. The van door was still tantalisingly open. Effie must have been thinking the same, for when Cait moved, her sister moved with her. Quiet as cats, they tiptoed to the back of the van. The smell was like heaven on a sunny day. Cait reached up and took down a strawberry. She gave it to Effie, then reached up for two more herself. They tasted every bit as good as they looked. Trouble was, as Cait knew, there's no such thing as 'just one strawberry'. Eating one or two made them want to eat more and in a very short time, Cait realised she had the husks of at least half a dozen strawberries in her hand. She was just about to throw them into the long grass, when she heard the farmhouse door slam.

'See you lunchtime!'

There was no time to run back to the water tank, and in any case, they would be seen. There was a gap just wide enough between the racks of strawberries, and quick as a flash, Cait and Effie had squeezed themselves in and worked their way to the back. Suddenly the doors were slammed closed, leaving them and the strawberries in the dark, and before they had time to think about what they should do next, the engine of the van roared into life.

'Where are we going now?' whispered Effie.

'I think to a market somewhere. That's what I heard the man say.' Cait reached for Effie's hand and squeezed it. 'Don't worry. We'll see when we get there.'

chapter eleven

The van was extremely uncomfortable. There was no space to sit down, so Cait and Effie had to crouch, which meant their legs went to sleep and they kept having to take it in turns to stretch out a leg, one at a time, to try and shake off the pins and needles. They'd eaten more strawberries of course, they couldn't resist them, but now even the softest, juiciest fruit had lost its sweetness. They were fed up with them. Added to which, some strawberries had jumped out of their punnets and as if it weren't bad enough being so cramped that there was only room for one of them to move one leg at a time, their fingers were stuck together with sticky juice and they could feel the squelchiness of squashed strawberries under their knees. Also, they had no idea, in this sugar-scented darkness, where they were. Cait reckoned the van walls must be insulated, as even the sound of the traffic she knew must be passing them was little more than a muffled hum. She knew then there'd be no point shouting out – they wouldn't be heard. 'We could sing,' she remarked, taking her turn to stretch out a leg. 'No one would hear us.' But the only song she could think of was an old Beatles' hit Mam used to sing, about strawberry fields, and she couldn't remember all the words anyway. Effie clutched at her as the van lurched and more of the fruit fell on top of them.

'Cait!' she squeaked. 'I feel sick.'

'Hold on,' said Cait, patting her back the way Mam would. 'We're nearly there.'

Disorientated, and not having a clue where 'there' was, they were both taken completely by surprise when the van suddenly stopped and the back doors swung open.

'What the ...'

Cait blinked in the sudden brightness. A man was looking at them in amazement.

'Did you ever see such a pair of strawberries as I have!' the man exclaimed.

Cait and Effie edged towards the doors. They must look some sight, Cait thought, with their strawberry-stained knees and faces. She dropped her legs over the back of the van. One or two curious market traders were making their way towards them.

'Quick!' she yelled. 'Run!'

Grabbing her sister by the hand, Cait sprang down and ran, dragging Effie beside her, faster and faster, until she was practically airborne. All around them market stalls were being set up. Boxes, baskets and trays of every sort of fruit and vegetable were piled high on all sides. Twisting and turning, side-stepping and swerving, Cait frantically kept herself and Effie out of arms' reach of any of the market traders, who were, by now, wide awake and in pursuit.

Ducking down under a cloth-covered table, scampering on all fours along the length of a row of trestles, then finding a moment of sanctuary behind the high side of a big yellow skip, Cait saw their chance to make a dash up a narrow street, away from the market, where the tarmac shone with rainbows of spilled oil.

'Where are we going?' puffed Effie.

'Anywhere,' panted Cait, dragging her sister down yet another alleyway that now echoed to the hollow sound of their running feet. 'We'll try this way.'

But the end of the lane was dead. High iron railings stood between them and rough ground on the far side. Cait was sure she could hear someone running behind them. She rattled at the railings, but it was no good. They were trapped. She felt like screaming, but she didn't have the breath. It was not fair. She kicked at the railings, and to her surprise, felt something give.

'Quick, Effie. There's one loose here. We could get through.'

It appeared that someone had deliberately cut one of the bottom bars, and then replaced it in the gap. It must have been someone small, for even with the bar removed, Cait had to twist her head one way and her shoulders the other in order to squeeze through. A couple of men had now rounded the corner behind them.

'Stop! Wait!'

'Leave it,' said Cait as Effie tried to replace the bar. 'They're too big anyway.'

Effie flung down the iron bar, and after wading through wiry grass and droopy-headed poppies, the girls scampered up the side of a mound of earth and stones and slid down the far side. They appeared to be on a building site where somebody had started something and no one had come back to finish it. Earth hillocks, their tops sprouting ragwort and white daisies, rose up around trenches, half-filled with blockwork and rubbish of every description. There was no one about.

Effie rubbed her arm. 'You nearly pulled it out of its socket,' she complained.

'I'm sorry,' said Cait. 'I just didn't want us to get caught.'

'I'm fed up with running, anyways.' Effie chucked a handful of small sharp stones into the air. Some of them hit an old oil drum that was partly hidden by a tall thistle. 'Will I see if I can do that again?'

'OK, but just one stone.'

Ping! Effie hit the metal.

Cait threw a stone and missed. 'Best of three, then,' she said.

They ended up throwing five stones apiece. Effie got three hits and Cait, four.

'Be a good place for a hut,' Effie remarked as they strolled down to look at their target.

Cait looked around. The area was already well used. What might have seemed, at first glance, to be an arbitrary scattering of rubbish, was actually ordered groupings of planks, metal drums and concrete blocks around burned-out fires. All about was strewn the detritus of human occupation. Empty cigarette boxes, plastic bottles, the charred remains of drink and aerosol cans.

'Funny place to do your hair,' Effie held up a recognisable empty can of hair spray.

Cait shuddered. 'Throw it away,' she ordered. 'At once.' There was a place like this near where they lived in Ireland. Kids used to come from all over to sit amongst rubbish like this. Talking and shouting long after it got dark. Dad forbade her ever to go there. 'Come on, Effie. Let's get out of here.'

Leading her sister by the hand, Cait almost tripped over

a pile of rags behind one of the makeshift benches – then nearly fell over in fright when the heap moved.

'Go away!' the heap growled.

'It's a someone!' Effie shrieked.

Cait tried to step back, go a different way, but her foot caught between two rocks and, twisting, she fell, her hands pushing out to save herself as she hit the ground hard. Red-grazed and stinging she saw jewels of blood burst on her palms, as instinctively she pulled her T-shirt down over her bum-bag. But it was too late. The 'someone' had seen.

'Got a fag?'

'No,' Cait said firmly.

'Money?' As the 'someone' raised itself up on an elbow, the rags moved with it. Cait took a step back, shielding Effie behind an outstretched arm. 'Wait. Don't go,' the man said, for by its shaggy beard, Cait knew it definitely to be a man. 'You *must* have money.'

Cait shook her head.

The man coughed. A horrible rasping cough that made his eyes pop and go red. In spite of herself, Cait couldn't take her eyes off him, or the rags that were his clothes, as they writhed and heaved. It was horrible. How could a man have got himself like that, Cait wondered. He'd be better off dead.

'Come on,' said Effie, tugging at her arm. 'Let's go. Let's get out of here.'

Cait took a step back and a searing dart of pain from her ankle shot up her leg. Her knee buckled, but Effie caught her arm. 'Come on,' she pleaded.

The man retched, a shaking spasm that ran through the heap that clothed him. He spat. A gob of greenish slime splattered a block of concrete – glistening in the sun. Cait winced.

'Now,' Effie implored.

The man looked at the two of them, his bloodshot eyes squinting. 'You've no money,' he croaked. 'No fags. What have you got?'

'Nothing!' Effie shouted. 'We got nothing!'

Steadying himself, the man focused his gaze on Effie, now trying to retreat behind her sister. 'I had a little girl like you once,' he said quietly. 'A little bitty girl with blonde hair. Just like you. Amy was what we called her ...' His voice trailed into silence.

'What happened?' Cait found herself asking. 'What happened to Amy?'

'Lost her,' the man said softly. 'Long time ago.'

Long time ago. His voice had an unexpected gentleness, like the beginning of a story Dad would tell her at bed-time. Dad could talk gentle sometimes. Long time ago. If Dad lost her and Effie, would he be like this? Ragged and wretched. Better off dead, her mind reminded her. Turning away, Cait lifted her T-shirt, unzipped her bum-bag.

'What are you doing?' Effie hissed.

At the bottom of the bag was Mam's half-packet of Polos. Cait took them out; slowly turned around; shyly offered them to the tramp. His eyes gleamed.

'Thanks,' he muttered, as she tossed them over.

The girls watched, as with his long fingers, the man scratched at the silver paper with dirty nails. He took one out – sucked it in.

'You want one?' He offered the pack back.

Cait shook her head. 'Keep them,' she said.

The man nodded. He seemed grateful.

A sudden noise made them all look up. A stone flew. Just a small one, and the man touched the side of his face where he'd been hit.

'Clear out!' a voice yelled.

Over the top of a pile of earth came the heads of five children. Then standing on the ridge, silhouetted against the sky, the tallest of them threw another stone.

'Get out!' he shouted.

Nervously, Cait and Effie began to back away, as, with a scattering of scree, the other children advanced.

A stout girl, her hair in rat-tail plaits, stooped for more ammunition, as the little girl beside her – a kid of about Effie's age, Cait thought – threw a bottle. Smashing, it exploded into glittering shards.

'Good shot!' encouraged her companion, lobbing her handful of sharp-edged stones.

In the sudden hail of small missiles, Cait and Effie tried to run, but for Cait, every step was painful on the uneven ground.

'Get out, now!' one of the kids screamed.

'This is our place!' shouted another.

More stones were thrown, but they didn't seem too close. The pain in her ankle was excruciating and Cait stopped, yanking Effie to a reluctant standstill. Why should she run, she thought. 'Face up to the bullies,' Mam had often told her. 'Show them you're not afraid of them. They'll back off soon enough.' Sometimes it worked, thought Cait. Sometimes it didn't. She turned slowly – they were only kids – she reminded herself. They weren't far away now – only about ten yards – and they were still throwing stones, and Cait felt suddenly ashamed to have run; they weren't even the targets. It was the man on the ground, now shielding his face with his long-fingered hands, who bore the brunt of their anger. This man who had nothing. This man who'd lost his daughter.

'Get out or you're dead.'

Huddled under his rags, the tramp crouched, head bowed; he seemed afraid to move.

'We'll make you eat dirt!'

'Leave him!' Cait suddenly shouted.

The stone throwing stopped. Five pairs of eyes swivelled round to stare, as Cait began a stiff-legged, hobbling advance.

'Don't, Cait!' Effie swung on the back of her T-shirt. 'Please!'

Outside, Cait was shaking with nerves, but inside, she was boiling.

'Leave him alone!' she repeated.

'Who are you?' the rat-tailed girl sneered, as if she and Effie had just crawled out from under a rock.

'Who are *you*?' Cait challenged.

'We're the Sharks.' Standing, with hands on hips, the girl tossed her beaded hair back over a shoulder. 'And we're ready to rumble.'

'You're bullies. That's what you are.'

The tall girl began to advance – a few slow, swaggering steps. 'Care to say that to my face?'

Cait stared straight into the other girl's cold grey eyes, but behind her back her fingers were crossed. A prayer flashed to her brain: 'Please God – let Mam be right.' The rat-tailed girl returned her stare, unflinching, but she stopped. She folded her arms across her wide chest. 'Who are you with, anyway.' She menaced. 'Y'know this is Shark territory.'

'And you weren't invited.' A scrawny, dark-haired boy came up beside the rat-tailed girl. He was close enough for Cait to see the still livid scar from a jagged cut down his cheek.

Cait tossed her head defiantly, pleased to see from the

139

corner of her eye, that under cover of their distraction, the tramp and all his rags were moving slowly from the hollow where he'd been sleeping. A little further and he'd be beyond an earth mound and out of sight.

'We're the Bandits,' Cait announced, hoping she wouldn't sound stupid. 'From Mexico. And we go where we please.'

'Says who?' snarled the tallest boy, tossing a fist-sized rock from one hand to the other.

No harm in names, thought Cait nervously, but sticks and stones break bones. Besides, there was no point staying around to get beaten up. The tramp was gone now, and it was a pity there was no one around to set up a similar distraction for herself and Effie. She took a slow step back, pushing her sister with her.

'Not so brave now?' The tallest boy moved closer; Cait could hear the thud, thud of the stone as he passed it, palm to palm. 'Where are you from anyhow?'

Cait hesitated.

'I said,' the boy was now so close Cait could smell his breath, 'where are you from?'

'We're from Mexico,' Effie had suddenly stuck her head forward. 'Like she said already.'

'Mexico, huh.' The boy was a good deal taller than Cait, his long shadow engulfed her.

'Take a hint,' the rat-tailed girl added her shade. 'Go home.'

'And don't come back,' the scar-faced boy added.

'Or else ...' Threatened a red-haired boy in slashed denims.

'Or else we'll beat you up,' squeaked the smallest kid, eyeball to eyeball with Effie.

'We were just going,' said Cait, with pretended nonchalance. 'Didn't think much of your place anyway.'

'Watch it ...' the tallest boy warned.

Already sauntering away, Cait tried to ignore the pain in her ankle. She must walk straight. Bullies, Mam said, went for the weak – the cry-babies – but she would be strong. Keeping close to her sister, Effie suddenly turned, then quickly and defiantly, stuck out her tongue. The smallest kid retaliated by throwing a pebble.

'Missed me!' Effie taunted impishly as she increased her pace to a trot, urging Cait to run with her. 'This way,' she encouraged. 'I think I see a gap.'

'Quick as you can,' Cait said. 'Run!'

Effie rolled through the hole in the chain-link fence quite neatly, while Cait had to crawl carefully through on her hands and knees. She didn't think they were being followed, but she couldn't be sure. They'd come out at a different place from the blind alley with the loose railing. This fence ran along the back of a line of houses. All identical. Even their back gardens were uniform in their overgrowth and rusting bike frames and pram wheels that pushed up through the nettles. Cait and Effie were in a strip of no-man's land between the wasteland and the back gardens. There was a worn track in the middle, as if it was well used as a shortcut, but even so, they had to fight their way through, with the thorns of bramble and blackthorn catching their hair and tearing at their clothes. Being smaller, Effie was able to worm her way forward faster, but with her ankle still quite sore, Cait soon lagged behind, so that by the time she emerged onto tarmac, there was no sign of Effie. For a moment she panicked, then realising that there was only one way Effie could have gone – the other being a dead end, she straightened up and limped as quickly as she could down the path Effie must have taken.

It was only a few yards to the end of that lane, and as she turned the corner, Cait was relieved to see her sister in the distance.

'Effie!' she called out.

Two infants, their fat-nappied bottoms grey from the dust of the gutter, looked up in silent curiosity, but Effie didn't seem to have heard. At any rate, she didn't stop or turn around. At least, thought Cait, she wasn't running, she'd catch up with her soon. Keeping her eyes fixed on her sister, Cait followed as fast as she was able. There were not many people about: a few kids pulling skids on bikes, a couple of dark-skinned women, their fronts bulging with babies in striped cotton slings, and an older woman, red-faced in headscarf and coat, struggling up the path, laden with shopping.

Effie made a turn, and as soon as she reached it, Cait did too. This next street was a bit wider than the last and further down there were shops. The kind of shops she and Effie liked. The ones with so much stuff in them that the moment the doors opened everything seemed to spill out onto the street in a colourful and haphazard display. Amongst all the people milling about, Cait saw her. She breathed a sigh, both of relief and breathlessness, for Effie had stopped. Dwarfed by a tower of plastic buckets and neon-coloured vegetable racks, she was peering in the shop window. Rubbing her ankle, Cait prepared herself for the last few yards to her sister. Then two doors down, she stopped. There was a man now talking to Effie. At first she thought he was just looking at the buckets or something, but with horror, she realised, when she saw him squat down on the pavement, that he was talking to Effie. He was wearing dark clothes; it could have been a uniform or something – maybe that of a policeman.

'Tell 'em nothing,' Cait found herself muttering, the way Dad would. She was too far away to hear what the man was saying, but she saw Effie nod once or twice, then shake her head. She didn't look like she was afraid – but Cait was. She was afraid that if she went up to Effie now and the man saw them together, he'd know who they were straight away – just like Col had. On their own, Cait reckoned, they might not be recognised.

Acting like she lived in one of the houses, or was just going visiting, Cait moved further down the street, keeping close to the wall. The man was still talking to Effie, but he didn't look up towards her. Effie mustn't have told him. Cait watched then as the man stood up, brushed his hands down the front of his trousers, patted Effie on the head, then went further on past the shops, hands crossed casually behind his back.

Cait tried to whistle, but even though it was more of a hissing snake kind of sound, Effie, coming back up the street, heard it.

'Go up to the corner and wait for me,' Cait whispered as her sister reached her, worried that the man in uniform might still be watching them.

'OK.' Effie skipped to the end of the road and at a discreet distance, Cait followed.

'Who was that?' she questioned. 'That man?'

Effie shrugged. 'I dunno.'

'What did he want? What did he say to you?'

'He asked me my name.'

'And what did you say?' Cait was alarmed.

'Told him my name was Ringo, didn't I.'

Cait grinned. 'What did he say to that?'

'He said "funny sort of a name for a girl". And I said I'm not a girl, I'm a Mexican bandit, but I don't think he believed me, 'cause he patted me on the head, and you don't pat Mexican bandits on the head 'less you want your jaw smashed in.'

Cait started to laugh.

'But he told me to mind now, and not be robbing too many banks.'

'That's brilliant,' said Cait. 'Absolutely brilliant.' She didn't tell Effie her fear of them being seen together, but suggested instead that they try walking down a different street.

'Which one?' Effie asked.

'Try this,' Cait said, pointing. 'See where we end up.'

After wandering for some time, they found themselves back on the street near where they'd started. The market was just a little way up the road. All the stalls were up and it thronged with people. Looking for bargains, Cait hoped, rather than them. Glancing down the other way, Cait saw a sign she recognised.

'Come on,' she nudged Effie. 'This way.'

'Where are we going now?' said Effie, wearily. 'I told you I'm tired of running.'

'You'll see.'

chapter twelve

Cait and Effie stood in front of the big glass doors of a railway station.

'We'll go by train,' said Cait, with some satisfaction, pushing open one of the glass doors.

'But, Cait ...' Effie protested.

'I saw the station sign down the road. Then when we got here, I saw the name. Bir-ming-ham New Street. Change at Birmingham and Crewe. That's what the man said.'

'But Cait ...' Effie had to trot to keep up with her sister, who, in spite of her slight limp, was now striding across the vast waiting area. 'Wait.'

Cait stopped. 'What?'

'Are we going to get tickets?'

'Of course.'

'What if the man won't sell you a ticket. Like last time.'

'I have an idea.'

'What is it?'

'You'll see,' said Cait mysteriously, as she strode off again.

To Effie's surprise, however, they passed by the ticket-sellers' booths and headed straight for the 'Ladies' sign. Wondering, but without saying a word, Effie followed her sister. At the wash-basins, Cait took a bunch of tissue, wetted it and scrubbed at the marks and stains on her face and hands. She made Effie do hers too. Once they were finished, Cait made Effie sit up beside the sink.

'Stay there. Where I can see you.'

'What are you going to do?'

'You'll see. It's my idea.'

With nervous fingers, Cait unzipped her bum-bag and peered inside. She took out her mother's-make up: the lipstick; the tinted cream; the eyeshadow and mascara wand. Effie's eyes grew bigger, but still she didn't say a word. With one hand, Cait held her hair out of the way, while with the other, she started applying creams to her face. Her hand was shaking. In her head she could hear Dad's voice roaring at her, the way he had when she came home from school one day with make-up on. Some of the other girls had done her up. For a laugh, they said. They'd painted her face with lipstick and eyeshadow and told her she looked cool. Cait thought she looked all right, but Dad didn't think so. The moment she got home he'd dragged her by the hair, screaming and shouting, to the bathroom.

'You'll get that stuff off, my girl. You're done up like a tart.'

After he'd scrubbed her face so hard that her skin was red for ages, he'd hugged and kissed her. 'You're my little girl, Cait. Not some painted floozie.'

Cait wasn't sure what a floozie was, but just now she didn't feel like a little girl, either. However, if it worked for Melody Smith, maybe it would work for her. When she finished, she turned to Effie.

'How do I look?'

Effie wrinkled her nose. 'Funny.'

'But do I look – older?'

'You look – different.'

Cait sighed as she lifted Effie down. She glanced in the mirror. She didn't *feel* different, but she hardly recognised herself.

They looked for the shortest queue at the ticket booths and stood behind a man with a battered leather briefcase. Two or three other people came hurrying to join the line behind them.

'Stay quiet and don't say a word,' Cait ordered as she dragged a £50 note from her bum-bag and held it tight in her fist. 'And keep your fingers crossed.'

All at once it was their turn. Cait stood up on her toes at the counter, so she would appear taller. She pretended nonchalance as she shoved the £50 through the hatch. 'One adult, one child, one way to Holyhead.'

The ticket man didn't even look up. He pressed a couple of buttons, printed out two tickets which he passed through the hatch along with the change for £50. 'Platform 6, change at Crewe. Next.'

'Glasgow. Return,' the man behind them called out.

The ticket man printed a ticket and glanced briefly at Cait, who, still on her tippy toes, was staring in stunned amazement. 'There's a queue here, love. People in a hurry.'

'Sorry.' Blushing at her stupidity and still stunned at how easy it had been, Cait grabbed the tickets and change. 'Platform 6,' she hissed to Effie.

The station was crowded with people. A few, sitting on suitcases, were staring blankly at nothing, but most were rushing, racing, avoiding the people on suitcases, their paths criss-crossing. Occasionally people bumped into each other and there was either quiet pardon-begging or loud cursing. Cait had a firm hold of Effie's hand, so she wouldn't get lost again or knocked down. Wishing she was taller, so she could see over the heads, she got caught in a tide of people, and released like driftwood thrown up on a beach, right in front of the row of platform kiosks. Number six, she saw, was just two kiosks down.

The man looked briefly at their tickets. 'On your left. Your train leaves in ten minutes. Change at Crewe.'

Our train, thought Cait incredulously. *Our* train. But of course it wasn't really their train, it was just a figure of speech. But for all that, it felt like it was their train – especially for them. Dizzy with excitement, she pushed Effie up the steps and climbed in after her. There were still plenty of seats, so they took a bench each, with a table between them.

'How long till we get home?' Effie asked.

'Not long now. This train will take us to Holyhead. Then we get the ferry …'

'Same ferry as we came over on?' Effie's eyes were shining with excitement.

'Expect so.'

'With all the games' machines and the drinks' place and the burger bar?'

'I'd say so.'

'I hope so,' said Effie. 'I'm starving.'

'When the buffet car opens, we'll get something.'

'What's a buffy car?'

'Place where you get food.'

'Were you ever on a train before?'

'No.'

'How do you know there's a buffy car thing?'

'I just know.'

'But how do you know when you haven't seen?' Effie insisted.

'I just do.'

'But how?'

'If you don't shut up,' said Cait. 'I won't get you anything when it does.'

Effie shut up. She was hungry.

The train was filling up now. People were squeezing past each other down the aisle.

'Are these seats taken?'

A man was asking. There was a woman beside him. Effie ducked under the table and popped up beside Cait to make sure she sat beside her sister, rather than a stranger. The man and the woman put the coats up on the racks and sat down opposite, just as the train started up, slowly gathering speed as it left the station. Effie and Cait looked at each other and grinned. The man and the woman were smiling at each other too. Then they started kissing and Cait looked out the window.

The woman giggled. She seemed happy. 'We're on honeymoon,' she said.

'Oh,' said Cait, not knowing what else she should say.

Effie said nothing, then scrambled up to Cait to whisper in her ear. 'If this is a train, why do they call it a honeymoon?'

'No,' said Cait patiently. 'They're *on* honeymoon. Means they just got married.'

'Why didn't they just say that then?'

'It's what people say.'

Effie was quiet for a while, but while Cait continued to look out of the window, she watched the couple opposite. 'I'm never going to get married,' she said eventually.

The woman laughed. A sort of tinkly-bell laugh. 'Oh dear. Why ever not?'

'Because,' Effie began. 'When you get married ...'

Just then there was an announcement over the tannoy. 'The buffet car is now open.'

Effie stopped whatever she was going to say immediately. 'There *is* a buffy car! Can we go? I'm starving.'

Asking the man and woman to keep an eye on their seats, Cait and Effie headed down the train. It was hard to walk with all the swaying and rocking, but they managed not to bump into too many people. Effie was disappointed they didn't do chips, but copied Cait and took a ham sandwich and a can of coke instead. When they got back to their place, the honeymoon couple asked them if they'd mind theirs while they went to get something to eat.

'Sure, no problem,' Cait said.

Putting their feet up on the seats in front and leaning back, they munched as the world rushed by the window.

'This is an adventure, isn't it, Cait?'

'Suppose it is,' Cait agreed, not knowing what else to call the nightmare of the past week.

'England must be where you get adventures.'

'Must be,' Cait humoured her.

'We don't get adventures like this in Ireland.' Effie pulled out a piece of ham and ate it. 'I mean, we do things. Like going to Nana and Granda. But that's not an adventure.'

'Aren't we going to Nana's now?' Cait couldn't help arguing.

'Yeah, but ...' Effie considered. 'We started from a different place this time. We didn't start from home, we started from an adventure.'

There was no arguing with *that*, thought Cait, taking a sip of her drink.

'When we get home, will Dad bring us to Nana's?'

It should have been an innocent question, but Cait froze.

'Usually he does. And will Mam come with us?'

'Effie –' Cait said quietly. 'They can't.'

Effie tucked a loose piece of ham into her mouth. 'Why not? Is Mam working?'

She wasn't trying to wind her up, Cait told herself. She wouldn't. Not about something like that. She *couldn't.* 'They can't, Effie,' Cait tried to engage her sister's attention. 'Because they're dead.'

Effie stopped eating and looked up, her eyes veiled behind her blonde fringe.

'And when you're dead – you *can't* come back,' Cait explained.

Effie's puzzled expression sought proof.

'Did Blackie come back?'

Effie shook her head. 'But we *knew* Blackie was dead,' she sighed. 'We saw her dead. I touched her. She was dead.'

'We saw Mam and Dad. I know they were dead.'

'*How* do you know? We didn't touch them. Did *you* touch them?'

Cait shook her head.

'So maybe they're not really dead.' Effie took another bite of her sandwich.

They *are*, Cait's thoughts insisted. I know they are. She tried to reason with her sister. 'When we got on this train, didn't I know there was a buffet car. Even though I'd never seen it – nor touched it?'

Effie nodded in solemn agreement.

'So there you are then.'

Effie shook her head. 'That's different.'

Why is it? How is it? Cait wanted to argue. But that

would lead to a fight, and there'd been quite enough fights lately. Let it go, she told herself. Effie could get odd ideas sometimes. This was just one of them.

'Cait?'

'What?'

'I've had enough of my drink.'

'That's OK. Leave it there. I'll mind it.'

Effie pushed her can up towards Cait's, wiped her nose and curled herself up on the seat beside her sister. Cait put her arm around her as the honeymoon couple came back. She closed her eyes and pretended to be asleep. She didn't want them to talk to her. They might ask questions. Effie was wrong, of course, Cait told herself. They *were* dead. You don't imagine things like that, do you? Even if at times she might have wanted them gone – when they'd be shouting and wouldn't shut up – when she'd be lying with her hands over her ears and her head under the pillow – she didn't *really* want that. She'd want them to be quiet, of course – to be like they used to be – but not dead. But they were dead, her brain insisted. You can't pretend being dead. Not like she was now – pretending to be asleep.

With a start, Cait woke up. She hadn't realised she really had fallen asleep, and now there was a man in a long grey coat, shaking her shoulder.

'Don't you have to change at Crewe?'

Cait blinked sleepily, wondering who this man was and how did he know.

'We're just coming into Crewe now,' and then, as if anticipating her question. 'I was behind you in the queue when you bought your tickets.'

Cait smiled. 'Thanks,' she said and woke her sister.

Crewe was a grey and draughty station and there seemed to be a lot of wind blowing in all directions. Miniature duststorms raced up and down the platforms. Cait looked around at the lines of trains, platforms, staircases and bridges. Change at Crewe, she thought. But how? Wondering if she would be able to make head or tail of the information board, Cait led Effie over towards the crowd of people already craning their necks to read the times and numbers. They didn't see the man in uniform until he suddenly stepped in front of them. Effie wanted to run and Cait was about to, but the man leaned towards them, like he wanted to be friends.

'Man in a grey coat said you want the Holyhead train,' he asked.

Cait nodded.

'It's OK,' the man laughed, noticing Cait's apprehension. He pulled at the badge on his uniform. 'I work here. I'm paid to help people.'

'Is that a job?' Effie asked. 'Helping people.'

'It is round here,' the man chuckled. 'Come on, I'll help you find the train you want.'

Cait looked at Effie and Effie looked back. He seemed all right, they were thinking, so they went with him up some steps, over a bridge and down the other side.

'Wait here,' the railwayman said, showing them a bench. 'It'll be the next train coming into this platform. About half an hour.'

'Thanks,' said Cait.

'I have to go now,' said the railwayman. 'But I'll be back when it comes in. Make sure you're on it.'

He did come back. The train had just come in and the doors were flung open.

'Safe journey now,' he said as the girls clambered aboard.

*

'He was a nice man,' Effie said happily as she threw herself into a vacant seat.

'I expect he gets paid for being nice.' Cait was cynical.

Effie stood up on the seat and looked around. 'Is there a buffy car on this train, 'cos I'm still hungry.'

After promising she wouldn't be sick, Cait let her have a sticky bun and another fizzy drink. She decided to have a bun as well, they looked nice, but feeling too grown-up for fizzy drink, she ordered tea for herself, and carried the polystyrene cup carefully back to their places. They drank and ate while watching the backs of houses and their long narrow gardens pass by the window.

'Are you going to leave that stuff on your face?'

Cait had almost forgotten she still had Mam's make-up on. 'I'll take it off.' She rummaged in the bum-bag for a tissue, then thought better of it. 'Maybe I won't,' she said. 'We still have to buy tickets for the ferry.'

The photograph caught her eye. The one of her, Mam and Dad, with Effie's knees being tickled. It was a bit scrumpled, so she took it out to smooth out the dog ears.

'What's that?'

'A photo.'

'Let's see.' Nearly snatching it from her, Effie peered at the faces. 'Is that me?'

Cait looked. 'No, it's me. You're the baby.'

Effie squinted for a better look. 'Who's holding me?'

'Dad.'

'Dad?' Effie questioned. 'He looks different.'

Cait studied the picture. Dad was laughing. Not just his mouth, but his eyes too. Maybe that's how he looked different.

'Who took the picture?'

Cait thought back. Trying to remember. Who was look-ing at them behind the camera? She remembered his voice. Cheddar cheese. Grease your knees. That's what he said. 'Uncle Robert,' she said. 'Dad's brother.'

'Dad had a brother?' Effie queried. 'I don't remember him.'

Cait barely did either, she realised. She had seen often when she was younger – and Nana and Granda always asked after him. He was a bit like Dad, but she thought his nose might have been bigger. The day of her First Com-munion was the last time he came to their house. He got into a row with Dad that night. The bedroom window was open and Cait heard them hitting each other in the gar-den. She'd never heard that sound before. Like slapping play-doh against a wall. Over and over. Over and over.

'Cait?' Effie was nudging her and Cait jumped.

'What?'

'That man over there. He keeps looking at us.'

'Which man? Where?'

'That one over there. With the sticky-up hair and checkedy shirt.'

Effie pointed and Cait looked. There were four men seated across the aisle. One of them had a blue-and-red checked shirt and blonde hair that stuck out all over.

'He's not looking now.'

'He was.'

From behind her fringe, Cait studied the man. He seemed ordinary enough. Surely nothing for them to worry about. Effie was probably imagining things anyway. Suddenly the man looked up. He had sharp blue eyes and all at once they were looking straight into Cait's. He smiled and waved.

'Howayeh,' he said.

A thought pierced her brain. Why is he looking at us? What if he's another man like Col? Col had a shirt like that. Cait felt uncomfortable. 'Do you want to move?' she asked Effie. Without looking at the men, the two girls left their seats and made their way down the aisle and into the next carriage.

'How far does this go?' Effie asked.

'Right to the back of the train.'

'Let's go there, so.'

They swayed and wobbled their way through carriage after carriage, until they could go no further. This last carriage had no seats. In wire compartments were stacked sacks and knobbly-looking parcels. Three bicycles, laden with luggage, were propped against a wall. A couple of odd-looking bits of metal stood in the middle of the floor, and in one corner, all by itself, a coffin. Cait looked away, but somehow it grabbed her gaze and made her look right back at it again. She wondered was it empty, or was there somebody inside. Was there someone down there lying quiet in that box, their face yellow and waxy, just like Nana's sister, Great-Auntie Kate that Mam had taken her to see in the dead-house?

'Will we go back now? It's cold down here.'

Effie didn't argue. She didn't say anything as Cait led her back through the carriages. There were a lot of people on the train, but they managed to find an empty seat before they got back to the four men. Checking that there was no one around who'd take any notice of them, Cait put her feet up.

'I'm tired,' she yawned. 'If I have a sleep, will you be all right?'

Effie nodded, and curling herself up as best she could, Cait tried to get comfortable. She unclipped the bum-bag and tucked it under her knees. 'It was cutting into me,' she explained.

The squeal of brakes woke them both up, for Effie had also crashed out, on her back with her mouth open, and Cait nearly rolled off the bench.

'Are we there?' Effie called out in alarm.

Cait scrambled to the window to get her bearings. They were stopped at a station, but from the hissing sound of the brakes they didn't seem to be stopped altogether. 'It's not Holyhead yet,' she said. 'The railwayman said Holyhead was the very last station, and I think we're moving again.'

The train edged forward, and soon they were off again, with the ground sweeping away from them in great green folds. Mountains rose in the distance. Cait settled herself back down again. Her feet kicked out along the bench, instinctively feeling for the bum-bag. They felt nothing. She sat up in alarm. The bum-bag was not on the seat. She checked the floor, even the dirty darkness under the seat, but there was nothing.

'Effie,' she said in a shocked voice. 'My bag's gone.'

'Gone?' Effie was flabbergasted. 'Where?'

Cait shook her head slowly in disbelief. 'I don't know. Someone must have stolen it. All the money was in there.' So was the photo, she thought bitterly. And no amount of money could pay for that.

Effie rooted in the pocket of her shorts and held out the few coins she found to her sister. 'Here,' she said. 'You can have all my money, if you like.'

'Thanks,' said Cait. 'But you keep it.' Her eyes felt prickly and she stared hard out of the window, feeling dangerously close to crying. Be strong, she told herself.

They were nearly home. She must not left Effie down. But, she thought, with a horrid hollow feeling growing in her stomach, without money for the ferry, what would they do now?

chapter thirteen

'Who do you think stole it?'
  'I don't know.'
  'Should we tell the police?'
  'Effie!' Cait stared in surprise at her sister. She must have sensed her desperation to suggest *that*. 'What would they do?'
  'Catch the robber?'
  'And then what,' Cait reasoned. 'They'd find out who we were. They'd take us away with them. Ask lots of questions. We'd never get back to Nana and Granda's.'
  'Suppose so.'
  'Aren't we doing all right as we are?'
  Effie nodded.
  'If only I hadn't lost my bum-bag.'
  'I'd say it was the man in the checkedy shirt,' said Effie firmly. 'Will I go and see?'
  'Don't,' Cait stopped her. 'It could have been anyone. And whoever it was – I bet they got out at the last stop.' She gazed at the sea which, except for a narrow strip of

sand seemed to come almost up to the train tracks itself. There were people on the beach: children, their parents, families. She sighed wistfully. It was as if the beaches in Cornwall happened another lifetime ago. She banged her head on the glass: once, twice. 'Why, oh, why, did I take my bum-bag off?' She banged a third time.

'Don't,' said Effie, reaching for her sister's hand. 'You've still got me.'

Neither girl said very much after that. They tried a half-hearted game of I-spy, but after guessing fields, grass, sheep and sea a couple of times each, they exhausted their repertoire. Eventually the train's progress slowed. Fields gave way to buildings, houses, yards and warehouses, until finally they were stopped and, in a mass of clicking, doors were flung open.

'Holyhead. We're here,' Cait said dismally, knowing there was still a sea to be crossed and no money to buy tickets.

They alighted on the platform and followed the crowds up a series of walkways signed, 'Foot passengers this way'. In a huge room with glass all around, they stood and let the crowd drift around them. There was a desk at one wall where you could buy your ticket for the ferry, but both Cait and Effie knew it was pointless to go there.

'If we walked in quick behind some other people, maybe we wouldn't be noticed,' Effie suggested.

'Don't worry, we would.'

Effie looked around. 'If we climbed into one of those big suitcases over there …'

'Now you're being silly.'

Effie went quiet; she hated to be called silly.

Cait wandered over to one of the huge windows. Out beyond the car park was an enormous white boat. Beyond that was the sea, and further than the sea, was Ireland. Although she couldn't see it, Cait knew it was there. And Nana and Granda would be there, too, waiting for them. Just then, Effie tugged at her sleeve.

'Cait, I just saw the man in the checkedy shirt.'

'Where?' Cait spun around.

'Over there,' Effie pointed with a finger held close to her chest.

Cait looked.

'He's been watching us. Will I ask him if he has your bum-bag?'

'No,' said Cait firmly. 'We don't know him. And, like I said, it was probably someone else.' She turned back to the window. The car park was full of cars, like a million shiny pebbles, glinting in the sun. There were some coaches, and …

'Effie, look!'

'What is it?'

'The jungly bus! Right down there, in the line of coaches.'

Suddenly the girls knew what to do. They ran back down the walkway, looking frantically for a way out. The first glass door they tried was locked, but the next one swung open. Cait ran for a while, then stopped; her ankle was still a bit sore. Effie was pattering behind her, trying to keep up.

'Come on, Effie. Hurry!'

Her sister's shoes were loose, flopping all over the place, but she was running as fast as she was able. Cait glanced up at the glass building and froze. The man in the checked shirt was at the window. She was *sure* it was him. Effie was right, she thought in horror. He *was* watching them. As Effie, panting, reached her side, Cait grabbed her hand and ran with her. The jungly bus was still a long way off, but the painted lions and tigers were growing bigger all the time.

'Wait. I need a breath.' Effie flopped, her head down.

Cait looked up, willing the bus not to move. It *must* wait for them. Suddenly she saw him! A small figure with scruffy hair and an over-large T-shirt.

'Storm!' she yelled, as loud as she could.

The boy didn't stop. He was too far away. He couldn't hear her.

'Storm!' she shouted again. 'Wait for us!'

Still he kept on walking, and faster now. He must have seen, as Cait just had, one of the coaches in the line was slowly making its way towards the line of ticket kiosks, towards the gaping mouth of the ferry.

'Storm!' she called, one last time, but the breeze was blowing her voice away up into the big blue sky. On the verge of giving up, she suddenly had an idea. 'Effie,' she said urgently. 'Whistle.'

Obediently Effie stuck her fingers into her mouth. She blew, and a faint wheeze came out. A real granny whistle. 'I can't, Cait. My puff's all gone with running.'

'OK, OK,' Cait crouched beside her. 'Don't cry. It's all right.' She tried to ignore the fact that Storm was walking away from them; that the jungly bus would soon be moving; that their chance would be gone. She tried not to notice all the other cars in this wide windy car park and the man in the checked shirt who may or may not be watching. This was just Effie and Cait. Just the two of them, playing a game. 'Take a deep breath, Effie. And try again.'

Effie breathed deeply, put her two fingers into her mouth, screwed up her eyes, and blew. The whistle was loud and shrill, long and loud. Mam would have hated it. Dad would have been proud. Cait looked up. The boy in the over-large T-shirt had stopped. He turned; he was looking.

'Storm!' Cait yelled, waving her arms. 'Storm!'

He saw them and he waved. Taking Effie's hand again, Cait said, 'Run now, run as fast as you can.'

Effie ran until her sandals flapped off and then she ran in her bare feet. She didn't flinch, not even on the hard gritty ground. Storm was all smiles.

'Can we ride,' Cait panted, 'on your bus?'

'Sure,' said Storm. 'But hurry. It's nearly going.'

The three of them fell in the door, just as the bus started moving. Deo and Rebus were sitting on the floor. They looked surprised to see them.

'We thought you had gone,' Rebus said.

'That the police had you,' Deo echoed.

Cait laughed, throwing herself on to a seat. 'We were too fast for the lot of them.'

Storm looked puzzled. 'Jason said that Col told him he saw you being picked up in Hereford. When we were at Uncle Pete's.'

'Col would say that,' Cait said bitterly, then, changing the subject, asked, 'Is my bag still here?'

'Under the bed.'

Just then Effie came out from behind the blanket curtain. She was cuddling a pink, fluffy rabbit. 'Mi Mi,' she said. 'He knew I'd come back for him.'

Behind the curtain, Cait changed, glad to get out of clothes that smelled of vinegar, wood ash and were covered in blotchy pink stains. She had one clean T-shirt left, and one pair of shorts. Feeling fresher already, she rummaged in the 'My Little Pony' rucksack. 'Here, Effie. You'd

163

better put on something clean as well. You'll want to look nice for Nana.'

'They won't let you stay on the bus,' Storm said. 'You have to get out on the boat. Mum says it's the rules.' Storm scratched his head, thinking. 'But we can't let her and Jason catch you, neither.'

'Why not?' said Effie. 'You said you'd ask him if we could come.'

'He said he was glad you were gone ...'

'Shut up, Rebus,' Storm tried to silence his brother.

'He said you'd bring trouble.'

'I said, shut up.'

'But that's what he said,' the younger boy insisted.

Storm grinned by way of apology. 'Anyway, it's better he doesn't know. So, here's the plan. When we're stopped, we'll get out – and you two,' he indicated Cait and Effie, 'wait a few minutes and come out after. Just pull the door and it'll lock. OK?'

Cait nodded. 'Will we meet up on the boat?'

'Where?'

'By the games machines,' said Effie. 'We know where they are.'

'Right then. All agreed? You two girls wait in Rebus's den till the coast is clear.'

The plan worked, and while none of them had much in the way of money, they contented themselves watching the flashing lights on the brightly coloured machines and imagining it was them and not somebody else that was at the controls.

'Where did you go, after?' Storm asked Cait casually.

'Nowhere much.' Cait was reluctant to say more. 'We got on a train.'

'And?'

'That's it. Pretty boring really.'

Storm looked at her from under his heavy fringe, but said nothing.

'Anyway,' Cait said, 'where are you going in Ireland?'

Storm shrugged. 'Some place called Awfully, I think.'

'Offaly?' Cait corrected, without thinking.

Storm looked at her quizzically. 'Do you know it?'

Cait reddened. 'I ... I just heard ...'

'We're getting a new baby.' Rebus didn't want to be left out of the conversation.

'Are you getting one in Ireland?' Effie was curious.

Deo gave her a withering look. 'How would we be getting a baby in Ireland.'

'We're getting it for Christmas,' Rebus chimed in.

Effie jumped, startled. 'There he is again!'

'Who?'

'The man in the checkedy shirt.'

'Where is he?' Cait tried to see through a gap between the machines.

'He just walked past. He looked in.'

'Who?' Storm demanded.

'The man that's been following us,' Cait explained. 'Since we were on the train.'

'I thought you said nothing happened.'

'Nothing did.' Cait cut him in two with a look.

'He stole Cait's bum-bag,' Effie said, 'we reckon.'

'He's a thief, then?'

Cait shrugged. 'He's been watching us. That's all.'

'P'raps he's a smuggler,' said Deo helpfully. 'With pocketsful of diamonds.'

'And racehorses,' Rebus suggested.

Deo cuffed him, 'Stupid boy.'

'I'm not stupid,' Rebus rubbed his ear.

'Not too bright, either,' Deo mocked him. 'Racehorses!'

'How would you know?' Rebus fought back.

'Look, you two,' said Storm firmly. 'If you're not going to stop fighting, go back to Mum and Jason. They're at the bar. Go and fight in front of them.'

Amazingly the two boys left.

'Come on, we'll ask Dad for a coke.'

'And maybe money for the machines,' Rebus suggested.

'Some chance.'

The man in the checked shirt stood out of their way as they left the games area.

'There he is again,' Cait hissed.

The man was definitely watching them, she reckoned. He seemed to be reading a paper, but she was sure his eyes were looking over the top more than at the pages.

'I'll go and ask him,' Storm volunteered.

'No,' Cait decided. 'We'll go out the other way. Go somewhere else.'

They went up the wide staircase to an upper deck and sat with their backs to a door marked, 'Staff only'. It wasn't long before they saw him again. Prowling round at the foot of the staircase, Cait was sure he was only pretending to look at one of the diagrams of the ship on the wall. While his back was turned, they slipped away again. They went round the little shop, round the dining area, even round a bit of the bar, taking care that Storm's Mum and Dad wouldn't see them. Wherever they went, sooner or later they'd see that familiar checked shirt.

'Are you sure it's the same man?' Storm asked, panting. 'That last shirt was red and green.'

Cait shot him a look.

'Lots of people have checked shirts,' Storm reasoned.

'Jason has one,' he ticked off his fingers. 'My Uncle Pete –'

'It is him,' Cait insisted. 'I just know it.'

Storm shrugged and, suddenly less sure, Cait took Effie to the bathroom for a quick wash under a cold tap. Looking into the mirror, she was horrified to see she still had the make-up on. It was smudged now and she looked awful. Scrubbing at her face with a wet tissue she wondered why Storm hadn't said anything. Maybe boys don't notice things like that, she thought.

'Now you're Cait again,' Effie said, approvingly.

For the rest of the crossing, they sat together in chairs you could lean right back in while, much to Cait's annoyance, Effie pointed out anyone wearing a checked shirt.

'Didn't Col have a checked shirt?'

'I don't remember,' Cait lied.

'They can't all be bad,' Effie reasoned. 'Not as bad as if they had a black hat and beard as well.'

'I know that,' Cait snapped back.

Storm had gone. He said he'd better go back to his folks, as he put it. Said he'd meet them back on the bus.

'But wait till the very last minute. So we can be sure Jason and Mum will be up at the front, ready to drive out.'

It was evening in Ireland, when the jungly bus finally rattled across the iron bridge and onto dry land. As the bus inched its way along in the queue of cars, Cait watched idly from the window. Around the terminus building, people waited in small groups. Families. All waiting to meet someone off the ferry. In the dullness of jackets and coats, her eye was drawn to a sudden splash of colour. A blue-and-red checked shirt! It *was* him. The man from the train. She knew by his sticky-up hair. All at once two small girls broke from the crowd and flung themselves into his outstretched arms. 'Maybe Effie was right,' Cait found herself thinking. 'They can't all be bad.' A woman in a pink jacket rushed up as well and suddenly the little girls were wrapped up in a huge hug. Arms around arms. Red, blue and pink. Cait found herself, arms crossed, hugging her own shoulders. Her mouth formed silent words, 'I wish.'

'Do you think we'll get to Nana's tonight?' Effie whispered.

'I don't know. Shussh.'

Suddenly there was an almighty banging from the front of the bus. Cait could hear Daisy's voice in an urgent loud whisper. 'Hide it quick, Storm. Hide it.'

Cait was puzzled. Surely Daisy didn't know they were there. She peeped out from behind the blanket, just as Storm came rushing in with two brown-paper packages. Rebus and Deo were right behind him.

'Hide!' Storm sounded frightened. 'Get under Deo's bed.'

'What's going on?' As the girls squeezed obediently under the bunk, Storm stuffed the packages deep into Rebus's bed. Rebus and Deo clambered swiftly into their bunks.

'Now, go to sleep.' Storm ordered his brothers. 'And don't move.'

Rebus and Deo closed their eyes immediately. Cait squeezed Effie to her.

'What's going on?' she asked again.

'The police!' Storm hissed. 'And sniffer dogs! We're being raided!'

From where she was lying, Cait could see nothing of what was going on. All she could see was dust, lots of dust, a dead spider and two socks rolled into smelly balls. With the tip of her finger she tried to roll them towards the wall – they were a little too close to her nose. She could hear voices: Jason's and Daisy's she recognised, but there were at least two more. She assumed they were the police. She lay very still and tried not to breathe. She heard the dividing curtain being pulled back and then she could see feet. Jason's toes were still hairy and very dirty, and the black shoes must be those of a policeman.

'These your boys?' It was a stranger's voice.

'Yeah. Deo and Rebus. Crashed out. Kinda tired.'

Cait imagined Deo and Rebus with their eyes screwed shut, trying not to laugh.

'And this is?'

'Storm. Our eldest.'

'Any more children?'

'Just three boys,' Daisy said.

Cait could feel Effie wriggling beside her. 'Lie quiet,' she whispered.

'There's something licking my feet,' Effie whispered back. 'It tickles.'

Just then a dog whined, and suddenly the blanket was lifted up, away from their hiding place.

'OK, you can come out now.' It was one of the policemen.

Sheepishly the two girls crawled out from under the bed.

'What the …' Jason sounded amazed. 'How did they get there?'

'Stowaways!' the first policeman exclaimed.

'Well, not exactly –' Storm mumbled.

'And you didn't know they were there?' The policeman with the dog was talking to Jason.

'I swear ...' Jason crossed his heart. 'But I think ...' he stared hard at his eldest son.

'I knew,' Storm admitted. 'I hid them. They were running away.'

'Runaways, so?' The first policeman sounded more curious than cross. 'Running from where?'

Cait and Effie stared at the floor.

'We're not running *away*,' Effie said in a very small voice, without looking up. 'We're running *home*.'

'Running home, eh?' The policeman crouched down. 'That's a different story. Let's have a look at you.'

Reluctantly the two girls raised their heads.

'Wait a minute!' The policeman seemed surprised. In fact he had to put a hand out behind him to stop himself falling backwards. 'I know you. Know your faces anyway. There's pictures of you two up all over. You're them Pengelly girls that disappeared after that terrible ...' He took his cap off and scratched his head. 'Which one of you is Caitlin?'

'I am,' said Cait. Looking over the policeman's shoulder she could see Deo and Rebus, their eyes squinting open. If she hadn't felt they were all in such deep trouble, she might have laughed.

The policeman stood up. 'Beats me how you got this far,' he said. 'We are out looking for you everywhere.' He looked at Daisy. 'Perhaps we should all go into the kitchen ...'

Straight away, he and the dog-handler ducked under the dividing curtain, with Daisy motioning Storm and the two girls to follow him. Jason hung back, leaned over Deo and Rebus and, as she passed him, Cait heard him whisper.

'You're still asleep. Remember?'

The boys jammed their eyes back shut and Cait joined her sister on the bench by the table. The first policeman was talking on his radio. Quietly. Cait couldn't hear.

'He's calling for back-up,' Effie hissed. 'How are we going to get away now?'

They sat quiet, while the police fired questions, mostly to Jason and Daisy. The dog lay on the floor, quietly regarding them, while its ears twitched, listening. Jason told them about the bus – that it belonged to his brother, that he was taking his family on holiday, that they were visiting friends in Ireland. He even told them about Cait and Effie staying with them on Dartmoor.

'But I didn't know who they were then, and that's the truth. I tried to find out. I swear we only kept them so they'd be safe. Until ...' he looked at Daisy. 'Told you they'd bring trouble,' he muttered.

'Two little girls,' the first policeman admonished him. 'And you didn't think to report the matter?'

'I told him not to,' Storm suddenly butted in. 'They were my friends.'

The first policeman smiled. 'I can see that.' He rubbed a hand through Storm's hair.

'Gerroff!' Storm brushed him away, sitting back and folding his arms. He glowered at the policemen, then at Jason and Daisy. 'They *are* my friends.'

'Well, I can see they've come to no harm,' the policeman laughed. 'And we have them now ...'

Effie reached out and grabbed Cait's arm. Her blue eyes widened with fear. Cait wanted to hold her, reassure her, tell her everything would be all right, but sudden terror had transfixed her.

A second before the door opened, the dog suddenly sat up, and everyone turned to look as a policewoman and another woman in a straight brown skirt came into the bus.

'Are these the girls then?' the brown skirt woman was smiling.

Storm kicked Cait under the table. 'Deny it,' he whispered. 'Tell her you're dogs.'

In spite of her nerves, Cait found herself grinning.

Daisy coughed. 'Excuse me, but what about us? We've a good bit to go and it's getting late.'

'We're going to take Caitlin and Aoife with us,' the policewoman said. 'Don't suppose there's any need to keep yous.' She looked for confirmation from the two policemen.

'We'll need a statement,' the first said. 'For our records. After that –'

'We will need to talk to you again,' the other policeman insisted. 'Where are you headed for tonight?'

'Daisy has family in Offaly,' Jason explained. 'We're going there.'

'Right so,' the policeman made a note on his pad. 'I'll alert my colleagues in Tullamore. You'll report to them in the morning.'

Cait felt, rather than heard, Jason groan.

'The first policeman nodded in agreement. 'Just a formality. I'm sure you've nothing to hide.'

Daisy shook her head till her earrings rattled, 'Of course not, Officer.'

Cait was positive she heard Jason breath a huge sigh of relief, but all he said was, 'That's OK then.'

'I'm not going anywhere with them!' Effie screamed suddenly. 'I'm staying here.'

The policewoman knelt down beside her. 'Why ever not? Your grandparents have themselves worried sick.'

'Is that where we're going?' Cait asked anxiously.

The policewoman nodded.

'You're lying!' Effie roared. 'You'll put us in a home!'

Caitlin explained about the last time, when Dad had tried to break the door down, and Mam sent them off with the police, and they weren't brought back for weeks. The policewoman stroked Effie's blonde hair. It was a bit matted now, with bits of stick and stuff, but it still made her look like a fairy. People always wanted to stroke Effie's hair.

'Is that why you didn't call us?' The policewoman looked up at Cait, 'Because you were scared of what we'd do?'

Cait stared down at her feet. Shrugged her shoulders. Mumbled. 'We thought you'd blame us.'

'Blame you! Of course not.' The policewoman reached for Cait's hand. 'We know what must have happened. We know how awful it must have been. We have to keep you safe now.'

'Like in a home?' Cait couldn't help the sarcasm.

'We won't do that. I promise. Your granny and granddad are waiting.'

'Nana and Granda?'

The policewoman nodded. 'You'd like to see them?'

Effie nodded. It was what she wanted more than anything else in the whole wide world.

'Cross my heart,' the policewoman said. 'You'll be seeing them.'

Effie was tempted. She looked up at Cait, who gave one of her 'what have we got to lose' expressions. Effie nodded again. 'OK,' she sighed in resignation.

The policewoman stood up. 'Will we go then, so?'

Effie and Cait got their bags and it looked like Daisy

173

was nearly crying when she hugged each of them. Jason seemed relieved they were going, Cait thought, but he looked sorry as well. Deo and Rebus were lying on the floor, watching from under the curtain, but as soon as they saw their dad was not about to be cross, they crawled out. The dog watched them with interest, and they stared back.

"Bye, Deo, 'bye, Rebus,' Effie waved shyly.

"Bye, Storm,' Cait said. 'And thanks for everything.'

'Don't worry,' he said bravely. 'If they *do* put you in a home, I'll come and get you out.'

Cait smiled. She leaned over and kissed him. Very quickly, on the cheek. Storm blushed, but, for once, he didn't try and hide it.

'Ready?'

Suddenly Effie turned from the door. She thrust Mi Mi into Rebus's arms. 'Here,' she said. 'Keep him for the new baby.'

Rebus smiled. A broad grin that seemed to crack his face in half. 'Thanks,' he said.

The police car was right outside, and Cait and Effie climbed into the back, while the policewoman and the woman with the brown skirt sat in the front.

"Bye 'bye, jungly bus.' Effie had turned to wave out the back window as the distance between them grew. "Bye Mi Mi,' she added softly.

chapter fourteen

They drove for a short while, and Cait had barely settled into the journey, when the car turned off the
road and stopped in front of a tall, red-brick building. The
woman with the brown skirt got out.

'Hey!' Cait was alarmed. 'This isn't Nana's.'

'It's OK,' the policewoman tried to sound reassuring.
'You'll be going to your Nana's. And when you've settled,
I'll come and we'll have a bit of a chat. Just a few questions. But it's getting late now – and we have to make
arrangements. You'll be stopping here for a bit. Mrs
Raleigh,' she indicated the woman in the brown skirt –
'will show you.' Reluctantly, Cait and Effie followed Mrs
Raleigh's brown skirt in through the glass doors, with the
policewoman coming behind them. It was a bit like an
office inside, but with thick carpet on the floor, it didn't
sound like one.

'Evening, Tom,' Mrs Raleigh said to the man on the
desk, as she led the children to the doors of a lift. The
policewoman stayed at the desk, talking to Tom. 'You're

very quiet,' Mrs Raleigh remarked as Cait listened in the cloistered silence to the soft thuds as the lift ascended. Thud. Thud. Thud, and the doors opened onto the third floor. Down a corridor, Mrs Raleigh unlocked a door. 'We've the best room in the house for you,' she smiled.

Cait and Effie peered in. Cream walls, brown floor and two pine beds.

'You said we were going to Nana's.'

'And you will.' Mrs Raleigh took Effie by the hand. 'You've a bathroom here as well.' She opened another door. 'All for yourselves.'

The bathroom suite was yellow. A sickly shade, Cait thought.

'Now,' Mrs Raleigh announced. 'I'm off to get you two something to eat. Are you hungry?'

'No,' Cait lied.

'No matter. Maybe you will be later. I won't be long.'

With a sudden click, the door shut and Mrs Raleigh was gone.

'Wait!' Cait sprang to the door, twisted the handle, twisted it again. 'It's locked!' she said in dismay.

Quick as a flash, Effie ran to the window.

'Don't, Effie!' Cait called out. 'We're three floors up!'

Noses pressed to the glass, they peered down. The window was directly over the main doors.

'There she goes.' In the cold greyness of the evening, Cait picked out the brown-skirted figure of Mrs Raleigh. 'She's crossing the yard.'

'She lied,' Effie said bitterly, turning away from the window. 'She said she'd bring us to Nana's.'

'She said she would.' Cait tried to ignore the lump of doubt rising in her throat as if to choke her. 'Maybe she will, later.'

Dropping her bag, Effie pulled back the sheet and climbed into the nearest bed. 'I hate her,' she muttered, curling herself into a ball.

Effie was crying. Cait could hear the unmistakable 'fffu-up, fffu-up, fffu-up' sound. She could see the bedclothes quiver. Taking off her sandals, Cait crept in behind her sister. Wrapped her arms around her, curved the length of her body about hers, stroked her hair. 'Don't cry, Eff,' she whispered.

The sound of the door opening surprised them both.

'Who is it?' Effie hissed, as Cait peered over the bedclothes.

'It's *her*,' Cait whispered back. 'That Raleigh woman.'

Effie responded by turning to face the wall.

'Good morning, girls.' She was wearing a green skirt today, Cait noticed. 'Trust you slept well.'

'You said last night, you'd come back,' Cait accused.

'I did. But you were asleep. Didn't want to disturb you, so I've brought you breakfast instead.' She pulled a trolley in from the corridor.

'What is it?' Effie whispered.

'Dunno,' Cait sniffed. 'Rashers and eggs, I think.'

Enticed by the smell, the two girls squeezed themselves from the bed. Each took a plateful of toast, egg and bacon. They ate hungrily.

'You must be starving,' Mrs Raleigh smiled. 'Anything else you want?'

'Only to go to Nana's,' Cait replied between mouthfuls, deliberately looking away out of the window.

'And so you will,' Mrs Raleigh assured her. 'Just as soon as you've eaten, washed and dressed.'

Cait looked down at herself. Her shirt, clean yesterday

morning, was now streaked with dirt from under the bunk and creased from sleeping in bed.

'It's OK,' Mrs Raleigh said, as if reading her thoughts. 'I've brought you some clean clothes.'

Curious as ever, Effie couldn't resist peering into the large plastic bag hanging on the side of the trolley.

'I've a lovely blue dress,' Mrs Raleigh said. 'Perfect for a pretty little girl like you.'

Effie wrinkled her nose in disgust. 'I'm not a little girl, and I'm not wearing no dress.'

Mrs Raleigh got down beside her. 'Lucky then,' she said, dipping her hand into the bag, 'I also brought a T-shirt and shorts. For a big girl, just about your size.'

Effie's smile widened slowly into a huge grin as Mrs Raleigh pulled out a shirt in two colours of blue and shorts so dark they were almost black. Cait found herself grinning too. Maybe this Raleigh woman was a bit nice.

There was a pair of cotton trousers and a pale yellow top for Cait. Not the sort Mam would ever buy, or what Dad would ever want her to wear, but it was just what she liked. Dressed up, she felt quite different – almost grown up. And with her hair washed and brushed till it shone, Effie looked good too. Mrs Raleigh had wanted to plait it, but Effie wouldn't let her.

'Leave it loose,' she pleaded. 'Not tied up like a baby's.'

At last they were ready and Mrs Raleigh took them down in the lift and across the soft floor of the lobby. Tom, behind the desk, waved, and as the big glass door swung closed behind them, they waved back. The car was parked at the front, and as Effie scrambled into the back seat, Mrs Raleigh asked Cait if she'd like to sit in front with her. She really was going to take them home, thought Cait, glancing at Mrs Raleigh's profile beside her as they sped away from Dublin, with the sun rising higher behind them. Perhaps she wasn't too bad after all.

The sun was nearly at its zenith when Cait began to recognise familiar landmarks: the cottage with the tin roof and a rust-stain shaped like a cat, the petrol station where they'd sometimes stop to use the toilet, the tree with one dead branch and one live one. Neither she nor Effie had closed their eyes for a moment the whole way. Mrs Raleigh talked a little. Asked them how they were, were they all right, but neither girl felt much like talking back. Most of the noise came from the traffic outside. Inside Mrs Raleigh's car was like a silent, sealed bubble.

It was only when they turned off the main road that Cait began to hear her heart beating. It began to thump quietly, a steady beat that gradually grew louder, reverberating right up to her eardrums. Louder and louder. Faster and faster. She put her hand to her neck; it was as if the very sound of it was trying to choke her.

'Are you all right, love?' Mrs Raleigh half turned.

Cait tried to answer, but when she looked up, Mrs Raleigh's face was distorted by her own tears, and she realised she'd been crying.

'Are you sure you're all right?'

They were passing the shop that doubled as a pub, round the next turn they'd be able to see Granda's chimneys above the high hedge and suddenly Cait wasn't sure about anything. She wiped her eyes on the sleeve of her shirt and Mrs Raleigh passed her a tissue.

'We could stop if you like,' Mrs Raleigh said, slowing the car to a standstill beside the rocky beach on the coast road that led to the Martello tower in the distance.

'Are we there yet?' Effie asked.

'In a few minutes,' Mrs Raleigh reassured. 'Your sister just needs a moment.'

Cait couldn't stop herself. In long gulping breaths she cried, while Mrs Raleigh passed her tissues, one after another.

'Why are you sad?' Effie brushed the back of her sister's hair.

'I'm not,' Cait gasped between sobs. 'I'm not sad at all.'

'Then why are you crying?'

'I dunno,' Cait mouthed. 'I must be stupid.'

'No, you're not,' Mrs Raleigh hugged her tightly. 'You're not stupid at all.'

Drying her eyes, Cait stared out over the dashboard at the quiet sea stretching away before them. 'Can we get out a moment?' she asked. 'Go down to the beach? I don't want Nana and Granda to see me like this.'

'Of course,' Mrs Raleigh assured. 'Fresh air will do you good.'

Her cheeks felt cold as the breeze dried them, and side by side, Cait stood with Effie on the sand of the little beach that had been their playground for so many summers. Effie kicked at the broken-down remains of a sand-castle. 'The Naughtons must have been here,' she remarked. 'They never could build a sandcastle as good as yours.'

Cait took her hand; small fingers fitting snugly into hers. 'We'll be able to build lots of sandcastles now. You, me and Granda.'

Kicking sand out of her shoes, Mrs Raleigh looked at them anxiously. 'Will you be all right if I go over the road. Tell you're grandparents you're here?'

Cait squeezed Effie's hand. 'We'll be fine.'

They didn't turn, but Cait heard her feet take slow steps in the sand away from them.

'Are there sharks out there?' Effie was gazing out to sea.

'Maybe,' Cait said. 'Long way out. But not near here.' Shielding her eyes, she scanned the horizon.

Effie looked the other way, out over the rocks that fringed the coast. Suddenly she tugged her sister's hand. 'Look!' she squeaked. 'There's Daddy!'

Cait turned in alarm. Way over on the rocks, a man sat, hunched. His black-shirted back was towards them. It looked as if he was smoking a cigarette, staring out at the waves.

'I told you he wasn't dead!' Effie called, breaking away from her.

Cait felt her heart lurch. It couldn't be. It shouldn't be. It *mustn't* be, she found herself thinking. Dad was dead. They'd buried him.

'Effie, wait!' she called out after her sister, who, running across the sand, had already reached the first of the rocks.

It *did* look like Dad, she panicked, stumbling across the sand and washed-up piles of weed. He was sitting just the way Dad sat that day on Spit Beach. What if Effie was right? What if Dad wasn't dead? What if the whole thing had been a pretend? Was Mam back in the house with Nana? It couldn't be that it was just Dad. Cait stopped. She was at the rocks now, but Effie was still ahead of her. Her head was beginning to pound, like her temples would explode. How many times these past days had she wished to put the clock back. A hundred? More? But what if it was only Dad who wasn't dead? Would he be just the same? Sad and angry by turns. What if he was worse? He'd hit Mam. That was the truth she'd never wanted to acknowledge. Who would he hit now?

'Effie!' she called again, her voice seeming faint.

Drowned out by the thunder of her brain.

Effie stopped. Maybe she had heard her, Cait thought, taking long careful strides across the rocks, keeping her sister ever in her sight. Or maybe there was something else. In sudden panic, she jumped the last pool and landed on the same rock as Effie. Her sister's eyes were bulging. Blue as marbles – blue as the sea – and wet. She turned them both to Cait.

'It's not Daddy.'

Cait looked. The man was watching them quietly.

'Hello, Effie. Hello, Cait.'

Cait's mind lurched. Remembering. Two girls. One in white. Smiles and laughter. Cheddar cheese – grease your knees. He *did* look like Dad – *and* his nose was bigger.

'Effie,' she said quietly. 'It's Uncle Robert.'

Uncle Robert stood up. He was taller than Dad, and thinner, but he had a kind face, Cait thought. He smiled – a nice smile, like he wanted to be friends.

'I've come to look after you,' he said quietly. He sounded like Dad. He had Dad's bedtime story voice. 'Me and your granny and granda.'

Suddenly Effie screamed. It started out like she was trying to say something, but ended up in a screech so loud it roused the gulls on a far rock into a whirling squawking frenzy. Cait tried to stop her, but she broke free, turned and ran.

'Effie!' Cait yelled. 'Look out! The rocks are slippy!'

But it was too late. With a thud and a strangled shriek, Effie was down, the screams turning to moans of pain. Cait scrambled to her side, but Uncle Robert was there first. She'd not even noticed him moving, but there he was, straddling the fallen girl. Reaching down, he scooped her up into his arms and Cait saw the jagged tail of blood smeared down the side of her knee. Staring hard into his face, Effie fell suddenly silent.

Cait led the way back across the rocks, back to the beach with the noiseless shadow of Robert and Effie sweeping over the rocks beside her. In the distance she could see three familiar figures come down the steps from the road. Mrs Raleigh behind, Nana and Granda in front. She waved double-handedly and they all waved back.

Then all at once, Effie started laughing, and Cait spun round in surprise. Effie was laughing. Stretched back across the arms of their uncle, her face red and pink with tears and smiles, tugging at the hem of her shorts and laughing. Then Cait saw why. Uncle Robert was tickling the back of her knees. Just the way Dad used to do. He was tickling the soft spots in the warm crease of her legs and Effie was laughing. He was laughing, too, his face that looked like Dad's face, now crinkled up and shining. With her feet sinking in the soft sand as she tried to walk faster, Cait began to laugh, too. Then, as if a cloud had let free the sun, she felt its warmth on her back for the first time that day. Arms stretched out, she ran the last few yards. Granda was there – Nana was there. Uncle Robert, too. They were finally home.